The

BIRTHDAY BID

Published by SDH Books
P.O. Box 340012
Sacramento, CA 95834-0012

Made in the United States of America
Cover Design: Sherelle Green
Project Editor: Paulette Nunlee of 5-Star Proofing
Interior Design: Milmon Harrison Designs

ISBN-10: 1-7337217-1-1
ISBN-13: 978-1-7337217-1-4

Library of Congress Control Number: 2019901621

The Birthday Bid is part of the Distinguished Gentlemen series

ALSO BY SUZETTE D. HARRISON

The Art of Love
My Tired Telephone
My Joy
Taffy
When Perfect Ain't Possible
Living on the Edge of Respectability

DEDICATION

This book is dedicated to my wonderful readers
who have gone the distance with me.
Bless you!

The

BIRTHDAY BID

SUZETTE D. HARRISON

PROLOGUE
Lexington "Lex" Ryde

Number twenty-one.

He'd aspired to many things in life, but being auctioned at a damn bachelor gig wasn't on his wish list. Still, Mama Peaches had left zero room for argument.

Time to give back!

His foster mother was all about the community. With Southlake Park in decline and the city too strapped to assist, she needed her beloved "gents" to step up and give back to the neighborhood that helped raise them.

"Let's make this coin and get out of here."

Exchanging dap with his "little brother," Adrian Collins, Lex was tempted to pay that base bid of one-hundred dollars twenty times over just to get ghost and be done with it. True, he hadn't been in a relationship in a minute, and a date—paid for or not—could be a sweet diversion. But, the idea of being "bought" had his midnight velvet skin crawling.

Eyeing the room, clearly some of his foster brothers shared similar sentiments. Only a rare, rogue handful seemed ready for the gig.

"Damn, I'm posted up on number twenty-one."

Being assigned so far down the list would make this night too long for his liking. Then there was the need to orchestrate a date with a stranger, which wasn't so simple for a man quiet and shy by nature.

"You better hope a dude don't bid on your ass and win."

"Aww, *hell no*, Adrian! You'll see a bruh walking up outta here."

Their laughter filling the air, he scanned the room again.

The place had power. Men, varying in age, whom Mama Peaches and Papa Brighton—God rest his soul—had raised filled the backroom, waiting to go on stage. Business owners, successful men, these Black brothers had been rescued from uncertainty and given a loving home in which to live. Not one was perfect, but Mama Peaches had raised them to be gentlemen. Now, they had an opportunity to raise this money and help her in a matter she considered utterly important.

It's a feel-good fundraiser.

Despite that mental reminder, his thoughts were already on his to-do demands. Mainly getting back to California, running a multi-million-dollar business, and living his best life that didn't include additional bachelor auctions.

Make it an adventure, Lex.

Sighing, he decided to take his own advice. Just as long as he wasn't bid on by a sister trying to be a wife. One wife in life was more than enough. He'd had one, and was done.

Sitting back, he closed his eyes.

Hurry up twenty-one, and let all shenanigans pass me by.

CHAPTER ONE
Senaé Dawson

Heffa, touch that blindfold and I'm coming out my neck at your expense!"
On the occasion of her fortieth birthday, Senaé Dawson was immune to idle threats. With bubbling laughter, she countered the warning from one of her trio of B.F.F.s. "Dove, sit your tired behind back and relax."

"No, boo, that's what you need to do." Ima's lyrical, accented voice floated from the opposite side of the limousine where she sat beside Dove, scheming. "Sit. Relax. And let us do this."

"I can't relax when I'm being kidnapped," Senaé jokingly complained, fiddling with the blindfold obliterating her vision. A hard slap on her wrist was her consequence. *"Ouch!"*

Seated next to her, Lovie rubbed Senaé's smarting skin. "Sorry, but we told you…"

"Don't touch the blindfold!" Three unified voices chimed.

"Seriously? Not one of you brown cows'll tell me where we're going?"

"Cows keep secrets."

Senaé laughed at Dove's comeback. "How about I throw out a couple of guesses. If I'm close, tell me I'm hot…or cold, if not. A concert? That new comedy club in the South Loop? Navy Pier for a dinner cruise?" Each guess was met by silence. "Fine! I'm not asking anything else."

"Good 'cause we're not answering."

"Whatever, Dove." Shameless in her cajoling, five seconds later Senaé ditched her own declaration to cease further questioning. Blindly, she felt for the hand of her seat partner, accidentally finding the valley between Lovie's thighs instead.

"Naé, we know you haven't had any in a minute, but I don't get down like that. Take your hand back."

Ignoring crazy laughter from the peanut gallery across the way, she managed to find Lovie's hand. "Come on, Lovie! Forget these cows and tell me something. Anything."

"Anything?"

"Yes."

"Senaé Dawson, you're controlling."

She snatched her hand back with a playful lip smack. "Forget y'all!" Crossing shapely legs, she folded her arms beneath her full-and-still-somewhat-firm breasts that were a credit to genetics, not her non-exercising laziness. "I'mma sit in this limo like a lady, but I'm telling you…when we get wherever we're going, if I don't like it it's deuces. I'm bouncing."

"Oh, trust, huntee! If things go the way we want, you will be bouncing courtesy of an overdue orgasm." Dove's pronouncement was met with high-fives and saucy agreement.

"Hush, Dove! I can't do you tonight."

"Yeah, but you need to *get done*."

High on birthday bliss and thankful for friendship, Senaé merely shook her head, ignoring Dove's standard out-of-orderliness. Over a decade of sisterhood with Lovie, Ima, and Dove had taught her some things: her girls were unpredictable when it came to celebrating. Forty, or not far from it, Senaé's crew fearlessly wore their Black Woman Magic. Their antics were never boring.

Sweet and semi-slutty, strip clubs and all things quasi-pornographic constituted Lovie's idea of birthday bliss. Ima, a Kenyan whose family migrated to America decades ago, was a hot, daredevil mess prepared to parachute from a plane as if guardian angels were her best friends. And Dove? The Chicago-born and raised cosmetologist was straight crazy. The end.

Calling their bunch lit, was a gross injustice.

And I love them as is, Senaé silently saluted, glad they'd survived the hills and valleys of life—laughable and otherwise.

Lord, I'm grateful to have these beautiful sister-women here to celebrate my fortieth circle around the sun. Let me survive whatever mayhem they've cooked up.

"So...where are we going again?"

"Naé, you're not slick. There is no 'again' when we never told your nosey bubble butt anything from jump."

"Please, Dove, just a hint."

"No!" was nearly shouted in triplicate.

"Now, take this champagne and kill the questions."

Obeying Ima's command, Senaé accepted the flute of bubbly placed in her hand.

"Toast, toast!" Lovie sang. "I'll start, and everyone else add on. Happy birthday to my beautiful sister-woman whose friendship I treasure..."

Ima's melodious tones took over. "Naé, we wish you love, the realization of your deepest dreams, and ultimate happiness..."

"And a big, rich, chocolate penis loaded with end-less make-you-pee-yourself orgasms." Dove's closure elicited screams of merriment.

"OMG, Dove, I hate you," Senaé hollered when her belly-aching laughter subsided.

"Yeah, yeah. We love you too, girl. Lift those glass-es. To the Queen of Shades!"

"To the Queen of Shades!" Ima and Lovie co-signed.

Hearing her blogger handle being lovingly hailed had tears in her eyes.

A licensed aesthetician and award-winning make-up artist, she'd worked her behind off building her business, her brand, and a social media platform and presence that had positioned her as a top beauty ambassador and trendsetter. Hitting over ten million subscribers last month, she'd danced around her living room wearing nothing but a G-string that nearly lost itself in her ample bottom. Her sister-women celebrat-ed her success because they loved her like that. Not to mention, Senaé's triumphs spilled over to Bella Noir, their co-owned full beauty business.

"Thank you, darlings, for making forty fabulous! So…is whatever we're doing tonight illegal?"

"Lord, this chick is back on it!"

"Ima, I love surprises. But I like being on the giving end of them," she reasoned, recalling their over-the-top excitement at her recent reveal of a once-in-a-lifetime opportunity to promote her own beauty brand offered by an internationally known cosmetic conglomerate. "Plus, this rolling blindfolded in the back of a limo is making me claustrophobic."

"Naé?"

"Ima?"

"You have one more time to question us and we will evict you from this limo right here *at night* on the South Side."

Senaé couldn't help laughing when Dove leaned across the aisle to pat her thigh. "So unless you packing a gat or have a wish to die, I suggest you shut up and ride."

Lord, I could be here, there, anywhere.

She was convinced her scheming sister-friends had commissioned the driver to take unnecessary twists and turns, defeating her attempts to gauge direction and distance. By her best estimates her blindfolded ride from her Bronzeville brownstone had lasted, give or take, a long and torturous twenty minutes. Despite wheedling and whining, she was no closer to solving her birthday mystery than when it first began.

Okay, I definitely have a new appreciation for the sight impaired. And, Lovie was a little right: I'm a teeny bit controlling.

She was a planner and a plotter who'd learned from life that organization fed stability, and stability tranquility. A loose cannon in her teen years, she'd settled into her adult self and had learned to weigh options before diving in. Just when suspense tried the threshold of her patience, the limousine came to a halt and its occupants sat in anticipatory silence. Bright relief sent her voice up an octave. "We're here, right? I need to see. Can I rip this thing off my eyes?"

"No, sweetie. It's on until we say otherwise," Lovie mysteriously advised.

Before Senaé could protest, cool night air rushed in as the rear door opened. "Ladies…"

Her life was mildly tame, never mundane; still, the

driver's disembodied voice produced a surge of adrenalin at the realization that—whatever her "brown cows" had strategized—she was about to get into it.

"Ma'am, watch your step."

"I would if I could," she joked as the driver assisted her exit. "Thank you. What now?"

"Walk slowly and obey whatever we say."

Guided by a friend on either side, Senaé complied with Dove's command. Cautious baby steps led to what she surmised was a sizeable building as doors obviously opened, treating them to a wave of animated, female voices.

"Ladies, welcome to Southlake Park Cultural Center, the home of tonight's…"

That's all Senaé heard as, what felt like, Ima's long fingers clamped tightly over her ears, impeding her ability to clearly hear. "What the…*Ima!*" Her attempt to escape Ima's hold was impeded by Lovie's anchoring arms about her body. "Okay, now. This is getting ridiculous."

Complaints ignored, Senaé felt herself being guided forward. She smirked, knowing a blindfolded woman being manipulated as if a marionette probably painted a picture of crazy or pathetic.

Their forward journey was brief. The shift in the air fed Senaé's assumption that they'd entered a much larger room within the facility. Loud music met her despite Ima's muffling efforts.

Whatever their location, the spirit was lively, boisterous, triggering in her a fresh rush of excitement.

Guided onto a chair, she felt about with her hands.

"Girl, stop before you knock over your water glass."

Chastised, she snatched her hands back. "Don't you think it would help if I knew our whereabouts?"

"How about Chi-Town?"

"Funny not funny, Dove."

"Hang in there, honey, the event's already on and cracking."

An amplified "Welcome to..." seemed to attach itself to the end of Lovie's pronouncement.

Hearing the emcee's greeting, Senaé was stunned. *"What?* Uhn-uhn! You heffas brought me to a *bachelor auction?"*

"We heffas did," Ima agreed. "And don't you dare remove that blindfold until we place and win your birthday bid."

"No, wait..." She wasn't one to judge but, in her mind, a bachelor auction was for the desperate. And that she wasn't. "I don't know about this."

"What's the problem? It's not like you gotta man."

"Well, dang, Dove!"

"Lovie, I'm just saying."

"What do you call Stanford?"

"A part-time penis."

She knew she was wrong for laughing, but her five-month relationship with the "part-time penis," Stanford Browning, had thankfully ended and she didn't miss it or him. A local morning show television personality, Stanford was all about image and appearances and lacked depth and substance in or out the bed.

That Negro was the most selfish non-lover I ever had.

"So, you in, Naé? I paid off my credit card and I'm ready to get back in debt just to buy you some dic—"

"Dove!"

"What? This ain't Sunday School, and none of you heffas is a saint. Besides, I brought back-up cash."

Based on the erupting laughter, Senaé was certain

Dove—her longest known friend in Chicago and mother of her godsons—had reached into the bra managing those 44F's to extract her emergency wad of cash. True enough, she felt the bills being waved beneath her nose, giving off Dove's signature White Musk scent.

"Smell that?" Dove needlessly asked. "It's the scent of success. I'm in. Ima's in. Lovie emptied the ATM. You in, Naé?"

Feeling giddy and grateful for women who loved her enough to do the ridiculous, Senaé decided. "In like Flynn."

"Then, woot woot! Let's do this!"

She was picky, and her girls knew it. Pickiness kept her from hastily repeating "I Do" after her first failed marriage; and reflected itself in Ima's, Lovie's, and Dove's lack of bids. While wild whoops and comical catcalls ricocheted around the room, indicating the desirability of the bachelors being auctioned, Senaé's trio of friends hollered along, but kept their cash close to their chests. They'd bid on only one bachelor but were out-priced by a woman who obviously had deep pockets and meant business.

"Ooo, Lawd, yasss! That's *the one*." Dove's response to the newest bachelor mounting the stage had Senaé sitting up straight as shouts and female appreciation for male fineness erupted throughout the audience.

"It's about damn time," she groused, having sat blindfolded through twenty bachelor bids.

"Girl, I wish you could see the walk!"

"Describe," she demanded.

"Swaggy, boo. Sexy. Panther'ish, but laid back. Confident. Like he's coming for you and you can't help but to let him."

"I need to see," Senaé begged, gripping Dove's arm as the emcee's hailing bachelor twenty-one as Ride-the-Knight unleashed wicked, wanton thoughts in her mind.

"Ride-the-Knight? Honey, we got car keys and condoms." Dove's quip left nearby ladies hilariously laughing.

"Jesus, if I wasn't married," Ima purred, "I'd definitely ride him."

"Lovie?" Senaé called at her friend's silence.

"Girl-l-l." Dove laughed. "Lovie can't talk for drooling."

Senaé's pulse quickened with piqued interest. "Describe him. Is he big? Motherland Black? Baldheaded?"

"Yes, girl, all your Mandika warrior favorites," Ima sang, "except the baldness. Low cut and lined."

"Facial hair?"

"Goatee and moustache. Nicely trimmed."

"Age?"

"Honey, melanin is magic, so that's anyone's guess. But I'd say mid-to-late thirties."

"Eyes?" Those windows to the soul were the first features on which she focused.

"Mr. Man has on sunglasses."

"At night, Ima?" She squirmed. "Jesus, he's a drug addict, or hiding something. Don't bid," she instructed.

"Too late," Dove advised. "We already have."

Through frenzied bidding, Senaé's heart raced. Her palms perspired. She tried getting her girls to back off as the bid mounted increasingly higher. Clearly, they were on a mission. When the auctioneer finalized what she felt was a ridiculous sum, her trio of sister-women erupted in victorious cheers akin to pandemonium.

Practically bouncing in her seat, she pleaded, "Let me see already!" The blindfold's removal left her blinking, eyes readjusting to light and sight.

"Sista, you better claim that gorgeousness before I do," a woman at a nearby table hollered.

"Honey, no. I said goodbye to thirty-nine last night. All that fine is for my fortieth," Senaé responded, provoking laughter amid hoots and congratulatory praise.

"Girl, go get your birthday boo."

Senaé intended to comply with Lovie's gleeful instructions, but was possessed by a temporary paralysis.

Lord, I must be pathetic 'cause I'm way too excited!

Focusing on the stage where her birthday bachelor waited, she felt caught in an immobile cocoon as she started at the bottom and worked her way up, delaying the pleasure of taking him all in. Slowly, her eyes moved northward. Her heart raced and her celibate cells were stimulated by the sexy sight of a tall, deeply dark, well-muscled brother dressed like he had taste, money, and maybe class. She savored the pleasure flushing her veins until her eyes reached his face, finding a far too familiar visage.

A multitude of seconds passed with Senaé sitting in frozen disbelief, mouth hanging open.

"Lex...?"

Eyes wide, she inched to the edge of her seat vainly convincing herself that who and what she saw wasn't real. Finding that man staring back at her, as stunned as she, Senaé wanted to scream. Instead, her frozen self defrosted when zapped by an unexpected lightning flash of lust that left her panties damp.

Head swinging side to side, hands swatting imaginary irritants, she confused her companions with hot objections. *"Unh-unh! Not! To! Day! Devil!"*

Pushing away from the table so wildly that her

chair crashed back, she didn't care. Disoriented, she was too busy trying to find the exit and hurry the hell out of there.

She'd reached the lobby when a hand clasped her arm.

"Naé, honey, what's wrong?"

"Let go of me, Lovie." Yanking free, she kept walking.

"Girl, you're straight tripping! You know how much money we just dropped buying that Birthday Boo? Senaé, bounce your bubble butt back in there and grab what we bought you."

She didn't slow as Dove moved alongside her—she and Ima firing questions. "Move, Dove," she grit when her B.F.F. jumped in front of her, blocking her exit.

"I'm not moving until you say what the hell's going on."

"Nothing's going on, 'cause I'm going home."

"Naé—"

"Dove, Ima, Lovie…look. I appreciate you trying to make my birthday special. I really do. But this right here? These random bachelor shenanigans? Not happening. I suggest you get a refund."

"All bids are final," Ima, the ever-practical money manager, provided.

"Well, I'll have to pay y'all back 'cause I will not, *cannot* go out with that man!"

"Why not?"

She stared at her sister-circle before—arms protectively crossed over her chest—stalking back and forth in a brisk, pacing pattern. "Because!"

"Because what, Naé? You're starting to scare us, and you're not making sense."

"Because…" A beautifully masculine baritone caused the women to whirl. Senaé's "birthday boo," the very object of her dismay, stood in their midst—calm, sexy, and collected. "I'm the ex-husband."

CHAPTER TWO
Lex

T*wenty-plus years! Two damn decades! And she still looks like the reason for my best erection.*

Naturally quiet, somewhat shy, Lexington "Lex" Ryde appeared cool, calm, and outwardly unbothered. Inwardly? He was hot as hell and fuming. Only Mama Peaches drilling into him that "challenges make you a better gentleman" kept him from going all out, acting ignorant.

"Lexington Ryde," he introduced himself to the women shielding his ex-wife as if he were a villain and she the victim. Ignoring the urge to turn over a table or two, playing the fool, yelling that he was the one needing protection from a woman who'd snatched out his soul and stomped it, he extended a hand. "Call me Lex."

"Oh, *Ryde* the Knight! Nice," the one introducing herself as Lovie practically purred, holding his hand longer than merited.

The tallest, bustiest of the crew snatched her back. "I'm Dove. That's Ima. Houston, we obviously have a problem."

"We have," he agreed, light brown eyes straying to his first love who'd become his worst misery.

Damn! She looks good!

Life had obviously been kind. She wore the heck out of forty, like it was twenty-five. That waist was still snatched. Those hips and breasts seemingly too round for her petite frame were even fuller, and still worthy of a triple-take. Those thighs that locked like a vise about his back during sensual rides looked yet firm and ripe beneath the fuchsia dress she wore like a caress. He felt a blast of heat he couldn't deny. Her high-octane curves had always been his kryptonite. But it was that deep down, chocolate brown skin; that Cupid's bow mouth made for licking and sucking that nearly lured him in. Almost made him forget.

Hell naw with this.

Shoulders squared, he shook off the enticement of her lips and thighs while refusing to meet those eyes that always weakened him, messed with his insides. Big, clear, lustrous baby doll eyes with absurd lashes she'd innocently bat and seductively lower when she wanted whatever she wanted. Back then he didn't have sense enough not to give in, no matter what it cost him.

I'm a grown ass man and that ish is finished.

Empowered by that benediction, he returned his attention to the mouthy one named Dove attempting to negotiate their current nonsense.

"...I'm sure if we find the organizers and explain the situation, they'll let us withdraw the bid."

Lex laughed despite himself. "You obviously don't know Peaches Brighton."

"No, I don't. Do you?"

"Yes." He left it at that.

"Well, can we get a minute of her time? We know it's a fundraiser, so we're not trying to be janky and steal back our commitment. No offense to you, but we need to work out some other option."

Never big on words, his counter was simple.

"Why?"

"Why!" was a singsong of disbelief from his ex-wife's women friends.

"Because!"

Hearing his ex's exclamation was torture and torment. Even so Lex nearly grinned, amused that she felt one word summed up the totality of their experience, or that one-word sentences were the only efforts she'd expend at his expense. She spat it like he was distasteful and answers were obvious.

"Because, Lex!" Moving from behind her wall of women, his ex-wife stepped to him, bold as she'd always been. So busy putting him in his place, she was oblivious to the fact that she was too up in his personal space, leaving their bodies separated only by air and an inch. "We're oil and water." Still that firecracker his younger self had crashed into love with, she stood glaring up at him like he wasn't a foot taller or a hundred pounds heavier, like she'd take him down if he so much as flexed. "We don't match. We don't mix. Is that simple enough without dishing all the business?"

Eyeing her steadily, he took his time agreeing. "It is."

"Good."

The finality of her tone, like she'd won something he wanted, rubbed him wrong. Annoyed, he slowly inhaled in an effort to keep his voice low and level. That inhalation created the opposite of its intended calm. Nostrils flaring with her soft, seductive scent, memories instantly flashed. He was suddenly eighteen to her sixteen, being worked over by what Mama Peaches would've called her "wicked wiles," her dabbing scented, edible "potions" on her pulse points and pleasure places for his consumption and enjoyment.

Like a fool, I ate that good and plenty at every opportunity.

Noting the rapid rise and fall of her breasts, feeling warm waves rolling from her skin, he wondered if she'd stepped into her own sensuous memory pit that she'd rather not deal with. He wondered if she recalled how they'd taught each other the art of tasting, the magic of motion, how to ride orgasmic waves wide as an ocean.

He shook his head, hard, flinging away fierce and fiery flashbacks. "Bet on it, BoBo, neither one of us wants this."

His use of the nickname he'd given her surprised them both, had them stalling.

"Do I detect an accent?" the one named Ima interjected in their tangled silence. Heads snapped in her direction. "What?" She shrugged. "I'm a foreigner. I catalogue differences."

"Lex is from Mississippi," his ex inserted, tone vexed. "Nice knowing you held onto something when you left so much behind to live that California life. Even if it was only echoes of your origins."

Peering down into those beautiful, baby doll eyes, Lex was dazzled by their angry lights. An undercurrent of pain mirroring his made their history all too real, too prevalent.

Rubbing a hand over his face, he mentally let loose an expletive, wishing he'd never let Mama Peaches talk him into this stupid-ass bachelor auction to begin with.

Lex was tempted to pull out his phone and take a picture for all his foster brothers' benefit. Mama Peaches, their steadfast matriarch and her ride-or-die

Miss Geraldine—two women who never experienced a lack of opinion—stood temporarily speechless? Only his ex could have that effect.

Tiny in stature, her spirit and persona had always been endowed with enormous impact. He'd experienced that magic when first meeting in his final season of high school football. Tonight was no different. The moment the emcee/auctioneer directed his sunshade-wearing gaze to the holder of the winning bid, he'd felt as if double-slammed by Tyson and Holyfield. Now, he stood, virtually TKO'd, needing Mama Peaches to get him out of this debacle and grant a second wind. Instead, she crushed his hope thin.

"Lex, baby, I'm sorry, but every bidder not only received but signed a copy of the auction rules and regulations."

"And I helped write them, so I know it was kindergarten-clear," Miss Geraldine added, fussing with her wig. "No refunds. No renege."

The Dove chick piped up before Lex could get a word in. "Ma'am, we're not trying to renege. We'll honor the bid—"

"Oh, I know you will, young lady! All winning bids are final and as is. Plus, we have your debit or credit card numbers on file and if need be, we'll charge them."

"Yes, ma'am, we understand. But—"

"But what?" On a different day, Lex would've laughed at Mama Peaches' comeback. "We ain't Jewel Osco's grocery. You're not buying and returning a bad batch of ham hocks and greens. How we gonna give back your money *and* rebuild the community?"

The one named Ima stepped up like some foreign ambassador sent to negotiate across enemy lines.

"Might I make a suggestion? What if you allowed us to transfer the bid to a different bachelor due to extenuating circumstances?"

"Baby, where're you from?"

"Kenya."

"Well that explains you thinking you can barter with me. This ain't no open-air market in the Motherland, so take a seat."

Noting the pimp-slapped looks on the younger women's faces, Lex slid between the two parties. "Mama Peaches. Miss Geraldine. Come with me, please?" Cupping their elbows, he escorted the older women to an opposite corner of the room. "Mama P., the ladies don't want a refund. They're simply asking to take the money placed on me and apply it to another bid."

"Lex, I'm up in age, not deaf. I know what they want and I heard what they said."

"We both did. Peaches, why my wig feel so wrong?" Miss Geraldine was still fiddling and fighting with an obviously new store-bought 'do, sitting on her head slightly askew.

"I told you to leave that synthetic mess alone and invest in human hair."

"Girl, Peaches, that Stemy is too expensive."

"I thought it was called Rhemy?"

"Rhemy! Stemy! It costs a pretty penny. Them wig makers won't have me so broke I'm sitting up cute and eating cat food."

"Lord, Geraldine, that cat kibble'll have you caterwauling in the choir stand." Mama Peaches' and her best friend enjoyed their jesting with belly-deep laughs.

Lex cleared his throat, steering the women back on track. "Mama P. Miss Geraldine. Can we do like the ladies suggested and let them re-bid?"

"Baby, business is business. You know this."

"Yes, ma'am, I do. But, you see what I'm up against?"

Their attention swiveled to the petite woman on the far side of the room. Perched on the edge of a chair—her profile to them—she looked at everything and everyone but him, clearly intent on avoidance. Appearing as displeased by the predicament as Lex felt, her foot tapped the floor in rapid succession, her body language tight. Tense.

Whoever said time heals all wounds was a straight up idiot.

Using her disinterest to his advantage, he leisurely scoped her, wondering what life had dealt her these last twenty years. Two decades apart and still this face-to-face dredged up their world of hurt that clearly hadn't healed. A man who preferred peace to conflict, this unexpected encounter had Lex feeling a whole lot that was less than pleasant.

Mama Peaches' light touch on his arm, redirected his focus. He looked at her with hope.

"Yes, baby, I see your challenge, and I can only imagine how you feel coming up on her like this."

Lex felt like that eleven-year-old kid she'd rescued from poverty and instability as her shrewd gaze swung back and forth between him and his ex, most likely missing nothing. Not the tension. Not the thing he'd been fighting and denying since seeing those kryptonite curves and familiar fire in baby doll eyes: hot sexual attraction.

His foster mother's strong voice was intentionally muted. "I wouldn't wish you a walk through that past for nothing. But…" Her heavy sigh was a precursor to an answer he didn't care to hear. "Rules are rules. If I make an exception and bend one for you, I'll have to bend them for anybody else dissatisfied with something transpiring tonight. I can't open that can of worms and create chaos when we're on a community-building mission."

Sunshades partially lifted, Lex lowered the depths of an already deep voice and gave his foster mother an innocent, imploring look. "Not even for your first and most beloved?"

"Ooo, Geraldine, you see this?"

"Yeah, Peaches, I see this big ol' handsome thing tryna charm you with them pretty eyes and the sounds of Mississippi."

Lex had to laugh. "Is it working?"

"No," both women answered before Mama Peaches took over, leaning close and quietly speaking. "Lex, baby, you were my first foster and God knows you have your own special piece of my heart because of that. Son, I'd do anything in the world for you…except this. That *South Side Weekly* photographer's here, and that little jogger—"

"Blogger," Miss Geraldine corrected.

"Yes, that. We're getting publicity, baby, and I'm hoping that'll keep the contributions coming in even after tonight. We can't afford negative talk of any behind the scenes shenanigans." She patted his face with tenderness. "And who knows?" He followed her gaze to the woman he'd married straight out of high school when they were both young and dumb. "That water

under the bridge might not be as troubled as it looks.
You've faced worse, Lexington. You'll get through
this."

I doubt it.

Senaé LaVonne Dawson was the one woman he
need never see again. And she'd placed the winning
bid? He'd worked too hard to heal himself; and had
no plans to take a trip back to broken. Returning
Mama Peaches' hug, Lex inhaled a cleansing breath.
Watching the older women walk off, he wondered
when God and the universe had decided he deserved
this kind of payback.

"Smile big!"

*Dude must be braindead 'cause ain't no way in hell
I'm smiling.*

Mama Peaches had done well in getting exposure
for the bachelor auction's community restoration
efforts, but Lex wasn't feeling this publicity nonsense.
Watching the photographer go in on his favorite
foster brother, Adrian Collins, and the sister-winner
of that bid, Lex was in no mood for grinning. He was
tempted to walk away and end the madness, but he'd
already been hustled up for a photo. He and the ex
were next.

I owe Mama P.

That truth kept him from rolling to his hotel to
sleep off this twisted predicament before hopping a
flight back to Cali. Loyal to the end, he leaned against
a wall, hands in pockets, ankles crossed, creating an
illusion of a relaxed and casual man. Only the twitch-
ing of his goateed square jaw hinted at the opposite.

Who is this woman, and why is she here?

Thanks to Adrian, he'd known about his ex being

back in Chi-Town. That truth never fazed him. His
west coast life made chance encounters nonexistent,
preserving needed distance. Now, here they were.
Same place. Occupying mutual space. What were the
odds of this nonsense? Common sense should've kept
him moving. Instead, he posted up, heart and mind
a warzone of fascination and resentment. The former
edged out the latter, leaving him staring, not caring.

The fact that she was still brickhouse built had already been established. Even so, behind the benefit of
sunglasses, he found himself neck-deep in assessment.

Skin dark like a chocolate bar, her makeup was
beat. Flawless. She was working the hell out of that
curve-clutching dress, silver statement jewelry, and
silver stilettos with rhinestone straps slithering about
her shapely calves. A short, spiky platinum wig that
might've looked ludicrous on another woman on
her proved gorgeous. She had "it factor" and carried
herself with alluring confidence. The more he stared,
the more he felt himself being reeled in by the woman
she was and the memories that hit. Memories of their
young bodies loving until spent. Recalling the taste
and texture of her magnificence, Lex found himself
suppressing a hot tightening and tingling in his south
side member.

"Can I help you?"

Realizing her irritated inquiry was directed at him,
Lex forced his focus away from her hips and slowly
traveled upward until meeting her eyes again. "Kinda
hard to help me when you can't help yourself. This
unwanted situation has us sharing a predicament."

"I'm talking about you getting your eyes off my
person and giving them a redirect. And what's with
the sunglasses at night? Are you a pimp now, or want-

ed by the F.B.I.?"

"Alright, BoBo, you got jokes."

"That and the need to be anywhere but here in present company."

Feeling dense waves of vexation rolling off of her, Lex chose to leave the insult where it lay.

"And let that be the last time you call me that."

"What? *BoBo?*" he couldn't help repeating, mildly teasing, earning himself a look that read, *Fool, don't try me.* "Fine, *Senaé*," he overstressed her name. Meeting her unflinching stare, he couldn't keep his full lips from grinning. "You grew."

"I'm still five-one."

"I meant out, not up."

"Bye, Lex."

Abandoning his relaxed lean against the wall, he sprang forward intercepting her departure. With a firm yet gentle grip about her elbow, he maneuvered himself in front of her like a human barrier. "Bo... Senaé," he autocorrected, "I meant no offense."

"None taken, Lex. But I do need you to move."

"I'm just saying, baby, you look *real* good."

"And I'm just saying this whole situation's bull."

"Maybe, but we're in it. So can we agree to civility for the next five minutes?"

"I'll give you four. Five is stretching things."

"Sir, you and your date are next."

Sighing, Lex acknowledged the photographer signaling for them. "Let's do this and be done."

"Let's."

With a gentlemanly gesture, he invited her to proceed, taking advantage of her leading position to scope her round, thick behind as if scoping was involuntary.

"Lex Ryde?"

"Ma'am?"

"Get your eyes off my assets."

Photo op finished, the blogger's chirpy questions asked and answered, Lex strolled towards the exit, Senaé sauntering sexy at his side but not fully present. As if her thoughts were scattered, and most likely, unpleasant.

At least she stopped the mock-murdering.

Through their brief, edgy exchange, she'd vacillated from ignoring him to dagger-glaring him to death. Now, as if relieved the ordeal had ended, she'd dialed down the hostility and was quiet, semi-human again.

"You still chew the inside of your cheek when you're deep-thinking or upset."

His stride slowed at her comment. "What?"

"You've been chewing that cheek like you haven't eaten since breakfast. You can relax now. We're finished. Good night and good bye, Lex. I wish you the best."

Walking in a hurry, she was steps ahead when his mouth got the best of him. "And our date?"

Lex watched the sensuous swish and sway of her fuchsia-covered hips as she moved farther from reach. "It won't happen. I'm donating my winning bid."

"So now I'm a charitable contribution."

"Call it a tax write-off if you will."

He felt an inner pocket of his suit jacket for his wallet. "I'll reimburse you for your loss."

"I don't want your money, Lex. And *neither* of us wants *this*." A backward hand motion indicated the situation they'd landed in.

"You're sure about that?"

He watched his words put her departure on pause. Confusion claimed her face when she turned his way, looking like she wanted to use the heel of her six-inch stiletto to whack some sense into his head.

"Lex, you can't possibly feel the need to spend time with me. Not with our broke down history."

Unable to account for his current stupidity—this sudden and defiant curiosity—he addressed the past. "We were young and dumb back when."

"True, and that state of ignorance left us suffering too many consequences that neither of us can afford to forget." She moved in his direction. "So, let's leave all this bachelor auction foolishness right here and let you do what you do best."

"And that is?"

"Disappear."

A fireball of anger and hurt burned through him. A child victim of abandonment, he'd never intended to inflict that same pain on them. Jaws filled with air, he tilted his head upward and blew a slow breath towards the ceiling before looking down into her eyes. He was surprised to find them shimmering, damp yet bright.

"You left me, Lex."

"Who left first, Senaé? You or me?"

"I moved to Dallas before you ran to California, but you know I'm not talking geographically, only."

They stood so closely he felt her warmth and her wounds. He silently considered her words. He didn't dispute her rendition of truth, rather honoring it even while offering his own. "That's not the whole story, baby, and you know it."

"Are you saying I'm lying and you didn't leave me emotionally?"

"I'm saying *we* left each other. Unfortunately."

"Unfortunately?" She cocked her head to the side in a way he easily remembered. "You have regrets, Lex?"

"Absolutely." He saw the light soften and change in those baby doll eyes.

"I do, too," she quietly admitted after a momentary silence. "We left some things unfinished."

"Such as?"

"Too many to count…but let's start with this."

Lex didn't flinch an inch when she reached up, removed his sunglasses, and licked her lips before pressing hers to his. Her lips were everything he remembered and obviously couldn't forget. Lush. Soft. Smoother than butter. But the pretty young thing he'd loved had vanished. A good God Almighty grown woman had manifested. Wrapping her arms about his neck, she slowly played that kiss like she was a musician and he her instrument.

Well, damn!

After all they'd been through, he tried not to feel anything warmer than ice. But parts of him missed the memo and responded in kind. Sensibility took a hiatus as heat crept in, warming him. Them.

Locking a hand about her waist, he moved so they were reacquainted form-to-form, flesh-to-flesh. When she didn't object to the tip of his tongue, he gently slid into her mouth, eliciting a sound he missed: her moan.

He nearly lurched forward when she abruptly ended their magic and pulled away as if embarrassed. "I need to go." In a hot hurry, she was halfway down the corridor before he recovered enough to protest.

"Senaé!"

She responded by increasing her pace, leaving Lex to hurry down the hallway. A large cluster of women headed in his direction interrupted his interception.

"Ooo, how *you* doing?"

He had to sidestep a sister stopping in his path, popping gum between gold teeth, her abundant endowment strangling a too small pair of leopard print pants, and five different shades of rainbow bright hair atop her head.

Easing his way around, his heart drummed wildly when realizing the one he pursued had cleared the exit. He took off at a jog despite an old leg injury.

By the time he navigated the human traffic in the corridor and made it outdoors, Senaé was long gone. The only movement in sight was that of a white stretch limousine leaving, its taillights like mocking red eyes.

Pacing a short stint, he let loose a low expletive. His mind locked onto a trivial detail as if keeping him from the real.

She has my sunglasses.

He needed them far less than he wanted her.

Feeling like the biggest fool ever birthed, he admitted what he knew when first seeing the woman who'd won his bid—long before the sultry benefit of her kiss.

Despite their past, Lex was still in love with his ex.

CHAPTER THREE
Senaé

S *alty.*
One word was enough to define her birthday weekend. Or better stated, her rank attitude resulting from it.

That limo ride home had been the longest of her life—drenched in friends' apologies, and her troubled silence. Once home, she'd locked herself in, spending the next day as a recluse bent on hibernating. She'd even opted for the livestreamed service rather than attending church Sunday. All because of him. Them. And the fact that she'd kissed her ex-husband. But could she really blame herself?

Her response had been honest.

I mean…for real!

That man was eye candy, wine perfected with time. He'd taken excellent care of himself over the years so that his NFL body was still hard and healthy. He'd gone from bad boy bald to low and lined, sporting a moustache and goatee with the finest sprinkle of gray that heightened his sexy. That sexy had her reeling, spinning all weekend, wondering why she physically responded to someone she should hate. Now, two days were gone that she couldn't get back and the salt in her 'tude was still on full.

Hearing a noise at the office door, she ignored Dove's entrance and her White Musk scent.

"Naé, your cell's rolling to voicemail. Your twelve-thirty called the shop phone saying she's running late."

While most competitors in their area adhered to a traditional Tuesday through Saturday schedule, Bella Noir being open on Mondays had given their full-service salon a leading edge. With Dove an expert on hair, Ima creating exquisite manicures and pedicures, and Lovie offering full-body massages, Senaé and partners had gone above the call of duty to ensure Bella Noir's success. At that moment she felt like dropping the ball, going home and crawling back in bed with a glass of chardonnay and pint of pecan praline ice cream for her spreading hips. Seated in their shared office, she offered a lackluster, "Thanks," but continued to pound her laptop keys—working on an entry for her Queen of Shades blog as if she hadn't heard a thing.

"Naé—"

"I got you, Dove! She's late. Okay?"

They laser-eyed each other as if hostile entities instead of sister-friends.

Dove was the first to break. Mouthy she might be, but Senaé knew Dove was never down for disharmony. "Listen, chick, how were we supposed to know who bachelor boo was when you never talk about your ex? *Plus*, he was before you and I even met, so other than that antiquated, faded Polaroid all crinkled and cracked at the back of your yearbook, I've never laid eyes on him. And he's obviously changed a beautiful helluva lot in the past twenty years." Dove closed the office door, ignoring Senaé's stubborn silence. "So, stop acting like it was some kind of intentional dis."

"Let's not talk about it."

"No, Naé, let's. Do you really think we'd do you like that?"

Saving her file, Senaé closed her laptop and inhaled a deep breath. Exhaling, she looked in Dove's direction without meeting her gaze head-on. "I kissed him."

"So? And? Did Armageddon happen? Are you headed to Hell?"

Senaé suppressed a laugh. "Hush, Dove."

"Girl, for real! You see how fine that man is? That tight, right NFL body. And the walk, Naé!" Dove executed a near-perfect pantomime of Lex's slow, sexy gait. "That excess swagger's carte blanche to coochie."

"It's a result of an injury, stupid. He has a rod in his right leg, and clearly learned to compensate for it."

"Who cares? He parlayed injury into *hella sexy!* So, yeah, I'd kiss him, lick him, dip him in white chocolate, start at his toes and eat my way up to his—"

"Enough, Dove. I get it."

"Apparently you don't and you didn't. If you "got it" we wouldn't be having this discussion. You'd be at home soaking."

"What?"

"Honey, soaking or walking wide-legged after getting whipped by that thick, rich Mandika warrior stick." Head back, body vibrating, Dove's simulating orgasmic sound effects had Senaé snorting with laughter.

"I can't stand you."

"But you love me and that's all that matters. Listen, boo, you kissed him. So what? I can't judge—"

"Sis, you know Lex and I have history that should've prevented me from even looking at the man." Senaé interrupted, shifting back in her chair as

Dove perched on the edge of the desk.

"Part of that history included sex."

"True, but we were young and horny then. I'm too grown to be playing the fool and giving into ridiculous whims."

"Were you good together, Naé? And you know what I mean." Snatching a pen from the desk, Dove pumped it between the open circle formed by her forefinger and thumb while sliding her tongue out her mouth and wiggling erotically.

"You've got to be the Devil's favorite daughter," Senaé joked, swatting her friend's thigh.

"Yeah, yeah. Were you?"

"What?"

"Good in bed!"

"Like I said, we were young and horny. All we knew was sex. We were each other's first, but we learned together and got it right. Eventually. Before we got married, we were always sneaking it in."

"And after 'I Do?'"

"We busted my full-sized waterbed. So, sure, the getting was good. Everything else we did?" Senaé shook her head. "Strong and wrong. That's why I spent my birthday weekend beating myself up over that kiss…and walking down memory lane, hating it *and* him."

"You don't hate him."

"What if I do?"

"You don't, and only want to in an effort to distance yourself from whatever it is you're feeling. You're struggling because you're human. And anal. And perfectionistic when it comes to you and what you do."

"Only a little bit."

Hopping up from the desk, Dove rushed towards

the door as if afraid to be struck by lightning. "The lies you tell! Naé, you're *the most* caring and generous woman I know. But you don't always extend that same generosity to yourself. I've told you before: you're too hard on you. I don't know everything that went down between you two, but you ain't the kiss-it-and-quit-it-kind."

Watching her friend open the door and stall in the hall, Senaé prepared herself for whatever Dove would say next.

"You're physically attracted to your ex despite the things you two experienced. If I were you, I'd run with that, and let the past be the past."

Dove's exit left Senaé mulling over words she considered beyond asinine and straight up stupid.

"Oh my gosh! Miss Senaé! My maternity pics are going to be epic!"

Feeling that quiet sense of satisfaction every successful makeover garnered, Senaé stood beside her seated client and simply smiled at the expectant, stay-at-home mother angling her head left, right, and left again—her disbelief captured by her mirrored image.

"That cannot be me."

"But it is, sweetie. Oh wait…no, boo boo, don't do it. Please," Senaé begged, seeing tears threatening to warp the hour worth of work she'd put in. "Lean your head back and relax," she instructed, grabbing tissues from her work station. Carefully dabbing moisture from her client's eyes, Senaé turned a cardstock advertisement into a fan with her free hand. "Take a deep breath. That baby needs oxygen." Her words had the intended effect of making her client laugh. "Let me get the camera and take your pic before the waterworks begin," she commented, spritzing her client's face with setting mist.

Emotions partially controlled, the young mother posed for the "after" pictures Senaé expertly took with the thirty-five-millimeter camera kept at the salon. She'd upload them—along with the "before" shots— onto both the salon's and her own Queen of Shades website when the day permitted.

"I can't thank you enough." Stunned and elated, Senaé's client continued admiring her transformative work before producing a debit card and paying the bill. "I feel like a different person. You're an artist, *for real.*"

Walking her client to the door, Senaé humbly accepted the compliment. "An artist is only as good as her canvas. You gave me the beauty to work with."

"My wedding photos don't even look this good," the young lady commented, catching her reflection in a mirror near the front. "Shoot, wait 'til hubby sees me. I just might get pregnant again."

"Girl, get out of here." Laughing, Senaé returned her client's embrace before shooing her out the door. Ignoring a delivery truck parking in front of a neighboring business, she returned to her work station and began the cleaning process. Sanitizing brushes. Discarding disposable palettes and plastic spatulas, she disinfected, sterilized, and reorganized—grateful to have gifted a young woman joy in her own image.

That's why I do this.

That joy factor was legit, and she loved seeing clients enter the salon one way only to leave enhanced by expertly placed "face paint." She knew that was too simplistic a description. Shading. Contouring. Highlighting. Balancing and de-blemishing. Taking what God gave and embellishing it to the nth degree. Transforming faces. Reaffirming intrinsic beauty. Once forced to mix the darkest of foundations with yellow and red tones to prevent her own face from looking ashen, she'd learned to blend palettes to suit deeper complexions. Having grown up being called "tar baby" Senaé made it her business to help Black women radiate the glory contained within.

God, I don't want to leave this.

Truly, she didn't. She had a steady clientele, a highly successful blog-slash-vlog, and had lent her expertise on several photo shoots for local magazines. She was content enough in each blessing. Yet, her pending beauty ambassador tour and collaboration would allow her new opportunities. God knew she needed something different.

*Not so much something…as some*where.

She'd fled Chicago for Dallas after her divorce only to find herself blowing back into the Windy City over a decade ago. She loved the nightlife and culture, but she'd tired of the icy winters; not to mention the ongoing, heartbreaking destruction caused by Black-on-Black violence. Might be a forty-year itch, but she was ready for the first tour stop in the Big Apple.

That's far enough away from California to calm your coochie.

Long ago, she'd forgiven Lex, but she'd vowed never to forget. So why had she permitted her defenses to slip in lieu of a kiss? It was downright ridiculous, and not the way to respond to one's ex. Fury and resentment were more understandable than intrigue, interest and straight up lustiness. But such was Lex: the first and only man to lead her to think with her vagina, not her head.

"That's Senaé right there."

Hearing her name, she turned to see Lovie entering the shop, holding the door for a delivery man.

"Miss Dawson?"

Eyes wide at the sight of an enormous array of pink gladiolas, Senaé offered a distracted, "Yes."

"Where can I put this?"

Indicating a cleared space on her station, she moved aside, allowing the younger man to deposit them. Taken by the delicate beauty of each bloom, she barely registered his, "I'll be right back."

"Girl, what you got?" Lovie and Dove lost no time peeking over her shoulder.

"Flowers," she absentmindedly answered, wowed by the glorious arrangement of her favorite florals.

"We know that," Lovie offered with a lip smack. "But who are they from? And what'd you do to get them?"

"I don't know, and nothing." Senaé's efforts to determine the sender failed. No card was attached.

"Naé, you have a mystery man?"

"This is the last of it, ma'am." Returning with a black box wrapped by a gold bow, the driver's entry interrupted her response.

Feeling oddly cautious, she eyed him skeptically, hesitating before accepting. "Thank you. Here…" Cradling the parcel against her hip, she felt distracted while digging in her wallet for a tip. "Thanks."

The driver wasn't even out the door before her girls pounced.

"Hurry up!"

"Open it!"

"Can a sister breathe a minute?" she retorted.

"No!"

Plopping onto her client chair, Senaé was deliberately slow in removing the elaborate bow.

"Girl, I'mma hurt you if you don't hurry up."

Shielding the box with her body, she blocked the one who'd moved in as if help was needed. "Back up, Dove! I got this." Her heart raced as she lifted the lid. Extracting gold tissue paper, she laughed when finding a crystal candy jar filled with her favorite indulgence.

"Black jelly beans?"

"*Yasss*, Lovie. You want some?" Senaé questioned, popping a handful in her mouth.

"Black licorice is not of God."

"Oh, but it is," she countered, eyes closing while slowly savoring.

"Must be from Stanford. His gifts *would* be late and lame," Dove complained. "At least he did good on the flowers. What's his card say?"

Thoughts of Stanford had her mouth twisting. The man had taken to blowing up her phone with calls and texts claiming a desire to "rediscover them." With his track record of multiple women, she couldn't pretend she was even—as her grandmother would say—a flicker-of-a-fraction interested.

Scooping up another mouthful of sugary treats, Senaé searched through layers of tissue paper until locating a greeting card at the bottom. Opening it, her eyebrows scrunched when finding another sealed envelope nestled within. She admired the image of a sister frolicking on a beach before reading what left her sputtering.

I didn't forget our date. Happy Birthday!
L.R.
p.s. Can a brother get his sunshades?

Coughing, she had to swallow hard to keep from choking.

"Here."

She accepted the bottled water Lovie pressed into her hand, and drank as if dehydrated.

"You okay?"

Nodding, she drank again.

"Well…what's in the smaller envelope?"

Ignoring Lovie, Senaé propped the box beside the vase of gladiolas, hopped from her perch, grabbed her purse and searched for her car keys, intending to leave. "I don't know. You can have whatever it is. But I'll take my jelly beans." Retrieving her crystal candy dish, she headed for the door, ignoring the sound of the second envelope being opened.

"Oh wow, Naé. Wait! It's a receipt for an electronic ticket!"

"That's nice. Enjoy it. And I won't even ask you conniving cows how Lex knew to reach me here."

"Don't blame us when your blog is always plugging Bella Noir. The man obviously did his homework. You don't care to know what the ticket's for?"

"Concert? Play? It doesn't matter, Dove. Lex and I aren't going anywhere or doing anything together. I'll be back before my next appointment."

Out the door and in the parking lot, Senaé depressed her keyless remote and climbed into her Infiniti G35, waving at the women hurrying her way.

"Forget those heffas and focus."

She had a blog entry to finish, edit, and post by tomorrow; social media posts to schedule, and tour updates to review. That in mind, she headed for Mocha Books Cafe to create in relative peace and quiet.

Turning on her stereo, she vibed to Kem, repeatedly reminding herself that Lex and his foolishness were not on today's menu.

A minute in, she found herself intentionally increasing the volume of her music in an attempt to drown out the constant chirp alerting her to incoming texts.

"I need them to quit."

She loved her girls, and knew they meant well. But sometimes they didn't know how not to go all in. Certainly, they wanted the best for her. Senaé had already decided that time with Lex wasn't it.

Finding a parking space, she slipped her iPad in her oversized purse and headed indoors. Ordering chai tea with milk and honey, she claimed a table at the rear of the quaint establishment and got busy with her blog.

She was passionate about Queen of Shades, and helping women of color celebrate their worth, having lived as a dark-skinned female subject to beauty prejudice and hurtful words.

You're cute to be so dark.

Her complexion wasn't a liability or a handicap. She didn't need "despite it, even if" compliments. Sipping tea, she shook her head at the dumbness. But such guised insults were insignificant compared to her stepfather's ignorance.

"I'm not raising some black ass nigga's blackberry baby. Who's going and who's staying?"

Her fairer-complexioned mother chose her man and shipped her only child, a thirteen-year-old Senaé, to her paternal grandmother in the Windy City. Initially crushed beyond reason, Senaé placed blame where it didn't belong until her Granny broke her off.

Baby, let me tell you something you may not want to hear. Your Mama's one of them women who can't be alone. She let you go and chose what's between that man's legs. That's her doing! Not his. And you better hear me when I tell you ain't nothing wrong with your skin. It's as smooth and pretty as mine is.

Her grandmother was a woman who sat in her "Black Beauty" like a queen without a complex. She taught Senaé that same self-acceptance. Fingers flying over her keyboard, her soft smile was automatic. She'd been blessed where others hadn't.

Too many sisters are walking around doubting their beauty...dark or not.

This was why her Queen of Shades work was hugely important to her. She was tired of sisters, women, feeling as if "not enough." Employing quick wit, offering amazing beauty hacks and tips, she'd parlayed her "problem" into a multi-million subscriber platform over the past decade. And now, she'd been offered the opportunity to take that wit on the road with a multi-city tour launching her own products. Granted the initial test run would be limited to five items, still she deemed it a monumental blessing. She had no qualms about re-booking customers with Dove whose aesthetician skills were nearly as good as hers. She'd even arranged to have live video streamed onto her social media outlets during the tour so as not to compromise her online presence. While ecstatic over new possibilities, she couldn't neglect the subscribers (male and female) who'd boosted her. She needed to stay connected.

So finish this blog entry...

Steely resolve kept her thoughts from wandering where they didn't belong. To a man. His unnecessary birthday gifts. And all that dark chocolate goodness.

Focus and knock this blog out.

Within minutes she finished. Feeling successful, she was determined to automate her social media posts. She could be completed within the hour if certain folks stopped blowing up her phone. Wireless earbuds in her ears, she accepted the incoming call with irritation and without identifying the party on the other end. "Lovie and Dove, I'm 'bout to kill a cow if you don't stop bothering me. What do you want already?"

"Hello to you, too, birthday lady."

She sat hypnotized by his lazy, liquid laughter that unleashed delicious flutters deep in her belly. Seconds passed in silence as she recovered her speaking abilities. *"Lex?"*

"At your service. Get your gift?"

Senaé stumbled over her words, tongue twisted. "What? No…yes…I guess. How'd you get my number? I mean…"

Get your life and put on some act-right, Senaé La-Vonne!

Her self-rebuke was effective, allowing her to deeply inhale a much-needed breath.

"I called your business number. You must have it synced to roll to your phone," he explained.

"Oh." Composed, she spoke calmly as if she didn't feel the man's sexy Mississippi tones down to her toes. "The flowers and treats were very thoughtful. Thank you."

"My pleasure, but those were appetizers. The ticket's the real deal. You accept?"

"No."

There was brief silence on the other end. "You're

not interested in a hot air balloon ride—"

"*Are you serious, Lex!* That was my gift?" She kneaded the bridge of her nose, suddenly annoyed. "Did you forget I'm deathly afraid of heights?"

His voice was low and slow when responding. "I remember more about you than you think I do. Like pink gladiolas, and black licorice. You love Alaskan Malamutes, and you're afraid of dolphins. And how you liked my licking that caramel-colored birthmark on your left—"

"Enough. I get it." She cradled her forehead in her palm. "You remembered some things…*except* that heights terrify me."

"Actually, I'm teasing. The hot air balloon ride was my original date idea. But seeing as how you won the bid, I changed it."

"To?"

"A train trip to California…something you always wanted."

CHAPTER FOUR
Lex

on't be the dumbest dude this side the Delta. Only a glutton for punishment would arrange a visit with his ex. But he had. Without thought. Because he had both means and motive. Now, he questioned the wisdom of it.

"Man, you did good. I'd want her, too, if I was you. She's smooth. Sleek. She handles curves like curves handle her."

"Yeah…got that boss beauty," Lex agreed, eyes on the road, expertly driving. "Deep black, onyx. Hot and satiny."

"You ride her yet?"

"Hell, yeah." He shot a glance to the rearview mirror for emphasis. "She hugs your stuff right. And she doesn't moan. She purrs." Lifting a fist, he exchanged dap with one of Black Hollywood's up-and-coming seated behind him.

"Money, that's what I'm talking about!" The son of a living legend, the young brother had recently filmed several performances proving his climb to stardom wasn't due to nepotism. "So…you're going to keep her?"

Accepting the phone being returned across the divider, Lex glanced at the photo of his latest crave before placing his cell on the empty passenger seat beside him. "I'm thinking on it."

"Well, I'm here if you don't want her, Ryde."

"Dude, your daddy would skin me dead."

"Last I checked I'm a bill-paying man."

"Yeah, alright, Little Prez," Lex offered with a chuckle, glad for the back-and-forth over a potential motorcycle purchase and the momentary distraction it provided. Lusting after a Harley was far safer than lusting after her.

I'm upholding my obligation to Mama Peaches. Nothing else.

Inviting his ex out west might've been considered an extravagant solution to their bid-winning date predicament. But nothing in the gesture was abnormal for him. Even when times were tight, he'd been generous. He wasn't a fantasizing man entertaining thoughts of happy magic and reunion. His motive was all about resolution. This gift of a trip was a peace offering as well as a whim.

Man, you're a living lie. You want to see her again.

There was that: what he considered an unhealthy interest. Their shared history should've squashed it. Instead, since their unnerving reunion and against reason, thoughts of Senaé came and went as they willed—frustrating, irritating, even warming and stimulating him. Intrigued, he was curious about the woman she'd become, and about her last twenty years. She'd obviously done well without him, yet she'd admitted to regrets. Had she missed him, them? Despite the remorse that hit the rare occasions he permitted himself to reminisce throughout the years, the idea that she might have similar sentiment felt foreign. In his angry pain, he'd written her off as cold and indifferent. Now, he felt himself softening as her admission of regret pulled him back to the truth of her essence.

One date. She bounces back to Chi-Town. And we're good.

"Money, you can't do right and call me something other than 'Little Prez?'"

Laughing lightly, Lex pulled his thoughts away from a woman who could easily become his crave. Again. His typical be "seen and not heard" standard of professionalism and rules against fraternizing with clients were relaxed in light of the fact that he'd known his passenger's father since Lex's pro-football days. Walking away from football after his injury, he'd parlayed the love for cars and driving inherited from his deceased father into a seven-figure business. Thanks to their past connection, Prez Senior had been one of his first ongoing clients. Lex "coming from behind the desk" and driving the family was further evidence of the long-standing relationship. "'Ey, blame your Oscar-having daddy for giving you the same last name as the first president of these U.S. states. Being his crumb snatcher, you gotta take the 'little' end of it. Know what I'm saying?"

"Yeah, aiight." His passenger's laugh was cut short by an incoming call. "Let me get this. It's my agent."

Nodding, Lex pressed a button, raising the soundproof, blackout glass separating the rear and front interiors of the black-on-black Escalade customized for the comfort and security of his A-list clientele. He'd never given a client cause to question his discretion. Unlike some in his position, he had zero interest in selling salacious information to paparazzi or the press. Brief though it was, his pro-athlete experience had enforced the fact that privacy deserved respect. He made confidentiality, unwavering integrity, gentlemanliness, and superior customer service the stanchions of his business. Those ethics had resulted in A Royal Ryde repeatedly earning high satisfaction ratings, as well as his being awarded Business Man of the Year by various organizations on more than one occasion.

God's favor is fierce…despite my failures.

Tuning into his world beats playlist, he was thankful and blessed to be an independent Black man successfully running his own small, but solid, gig.

Nothing small about a fleet of a dozen.

He knew companies whose fleets exceeded one hundred. But those were corporate, whereas he was grassroots. Or as he liked to say "built from the bottom." Pristine and parked in assigned slots in what resembled a large airplane hangar, sat his vehicles not currently in use. After a series of thefts and vandalism, Lex had opted to relocate to an indoor set-up with iron gates about the perimeter and twenty-four-hour security on the premises. Sedans, SUVs, a Hummer, a party bus, two stretch and a super stretch limousine comprised the bulk of his black-on-black twelve-vehicle fleet. But it was the vintage pearl-colored Phantom Rolls Royce and caramel-on-bronze Bentley that thrilled him bone-deep.

He'd sunk a grip into customizing the entire fleet to suit his clientele's needs. The investment had been worth it. Captain chairs. Black out glass. Smoked glass partitions, telephones and intercoms. Reclining seats, extra leg room, satellite and direct television were amenities he offered so that his fleet essentially proved to be mobile offices. Or as his administrative assistant, Kayla, liked to say, they offered "the comforts of home in a car." As his admin, Kayla was an expert in catering to the creature comforts of every customer—be it champagne, flowers, gourmet chocolates, or water costing ten dollars a bottle. She and her part-time personal assistant Lex insisted on hiring as business exploded, ensured every vehicle was well-stocked to satisfy the whims and the wants. A Royal Ryde went above and beyond the call of duty, cementing their success despite the lower priced ride-share phenomenon that had threatened to be a thorn in his side. Initial concerns had proven unnecessary. The loyalty of his customer base and their preference for his services was astounding.

Twenty years in the industry and he'd grown from hustling rides on the side to a seven-figure business with a cadre of clients ranging from actors, producers, politicians, rappers and singers, comedians and professional athletes who contracted Lex's services not only for themselves but their families. A Royal Ryde had become the go-to transportation service catering to Hollywood's and the entertainment industry's African American royalty. At the end of the day he was pleased and had no need to compare his progress with corporate giants. Success was relative. And his was good.

Smoothly navigating onto the freeway, he glanced at the dashboard clock and was satisfied to see he was on schedule. Thanks to L.A.'s notoriously crazy traffic situations, he habitually allowed for mishaps and unexpected delays. Being prompt and on point was another basic tenet of his success.

None of that CPT, he silently joked, recalling Mama Peaches' perpetual jest about folks prone to operate on Colored People's Time running around like headless chickens at Judgement.

"You watch! When the Rapture happens some folks gonna get locked outside the pearly gates for strolling up twenty minutes after the trumpet blast, talking 'bout, "I been late to church every Sunday of my life, Lord, and You never objected. Jesus, I'm just saying!"'

Laughing, he needlessly checked the time again while cautioning himself to relax. This charity event sponsored by some of Black Hollywood's hottest would get a brief appearance from Little Prez before the man had to bounce for a scheduled flight out of Burbank. After safely transporting his passenger? Lex was headed for Amtrak. And his ex.

I'm still wigging out that she changed up and accepted.

His disbelief was even greater over the fact that he'd had the ignorant idea to begin with.

It had been a shot in the dark: that ticket. He still second-guessed its gifting. He was quick about his business, but not necessarily spontaneous or given to randomness. Clearly, a date wasn't desired. That didn't prevent him from being extreme in executing it.

But why?

Stubbornness? Stupidity?

Lex decided it was a little of each. Naturally competitive, the retired athlete in him was about not just the game, but the win. He wasn't interested in chasing his ex, or gaming up anything that remotely smelled like romance. The win he wanted was pure and simple. He wanted Senaé's forgiveness.

Rag'n'Bone Man's "*Humam*" chose that moment to pump into the rotation as if underscoring Lex's sentiment. Only regard for his client kept him from putting the volume on blast. The song's driving rhythm and bass were tight, the message right. He was human. And in his humanness his initial negative reaction to his ex's falling into his presence had been from the gut, truly foul and less than effervescent. But life had whipped one lesson upside his head: be better, not bitter. Perhaps this asinine invitation was some perverse challenge, a means of gauging whether or not she was open to healing their past.

The Escalade's buzzing phone interrupted his thoughts. He answered, showing the respect he would any client. "Yes, sir?"

"*Man*, Money! The ish—"

"You alright?" His client's tone had Lex glancing in the rearview mirror despite the glass partition, unclear about the source of the obvious annoyance and whether it was minor or cause for his concealed weapon. Lex knew not to overreact, but in his line of business he'd encountered threats to the safe transport of his clients. Paparazzi. Overzealous, idiot fans. Even rival adversaries aimed at vengeful get-back. Depending on the caliber of his client, he was known to ride with security detail in the vehicle with him; or even escorted by security in a vehicle before and a vehicle behind. He'd completed aggressive driving courses to aid in avoiding paparazzi, or prevent being boxed in by imminent threats. Regardless of the extent of such safety measures, Lex was bonded and licensed to carry a concealed weapon and while on duty was always strapped and "ready to resolve."

Little Prez's stingy laugh lessened Lex's heightened alert. "Sorry for sounding all alarming. I have a simple situation called a change of plans. My agent moved some things and is just now informing me. He has me on an earlier flight for filming, so I'mma hit this charity event only a quick minute before I have to float to LAX instead of Burbank. Can you roll with me on that?"

"Yes, sir," Lex assured, disconnecting before mentally ripping an expletive. The change in airports would take him in a direction opposite of Amtrak, and onto a freeway he jokingly had a personal vendetta against.

Day or night, traffic on the 405 is a beast and a bitch.

Meeting Senaé's train on time would prove more an impossibility than a stretch. He couldn't afford to be late on a woman whose memory bank already tagged him as an undependable flake. He had to insert Plan B in his game.

Eleven o'clock at night or not, a group of street performers was still doing their thing entertaining and money hustling. Giving them a wide berth, Lex hurried through traveling masses wishing his sprint and dash were still on point. Instead, he was forced to adapt a light jog thanks to the surgical rod in his leg that had never healed to his complete satisfaction.

"Khaleed!"

Decked in uniform same as Lex—black suit, cap, and signature gold tie—his top employee and right-hand man wasn't far ahead. "Hey, Boss."

Slightly winded, Lex caught his breath before exchanging dap with the younger man. "Thanks for covering."

"Most def. I got you like you got me," Khaleed stated, forever reminding Lex that his giving the high school drop-out a chance when other employers failed to had earned his absolute loyalty.

"She hasn't come through yet?" Lex vainly scanned the surrounding vicinity, coming up empty.

"Boss Man, I've been posted up holding this high

since before the train arrived." Khaleed waved an over-sized sign bearing the words "Miss Dawson" in huge type. "And nothing. Not one sister fitting her description. But I did see this fine ass honey—"

"'Ey, off site or not, you're still on duty," Lex reminded, serious about his no profanity policy while working.

"All I'm saying is she was a fine bitc—"

Lex lifting his sunglasses to spear Khaleed with a keep-playing-with-me-and-see look left the younger man laughing.

"I'm joking."

"You gonna be joking in the jobless line," Lex cautioned, knowing it would take a greater offense to justify Khaleed's termination. Lex had instantly bonded with the high school drop-out who'd spent time in juvenile hall and foster care when he'd shown up nine years ago asking if he could earn a few dollars washing cars for A Royal Ryde. Living "from sofa to sofa" after an eighteen-month conviction for possession of three joints, Khaleed had failed to finish high school and struggled in the face of unemployment. His response to Lex's inquiry as to how the young man planned to spend his earnings had sealed the deal.

My baby sister, Kayla's, still in the system, and I'm not liking or trusting that foster family dad. I gotta do what I do to get her outta there and make a way for us.

Lex knew Heaven had smiled on him when his mother left him asleep on a church pew at the end of a prayer service and walked away with his four younger siblings. Papa Brighton's acting as church custodian and finding the slumbering eleven-year-old and taking him home to his wife, Mama Peaches, when mental illness took Lex's mother down a path of no return, spared Lex horrors unknown. Hearing Khaleed's story and seeing his determination, as the oldest son Lex understood his need to protect his sister. Still, Lex tested him, assigning Khaleed the task of washing his, then, fleet of four in under sixty minutes.

"I can do that, Mr. Ryde, but if you want it done right, I'mma need to take my time."

That turned all tables in Khaleed's favor. Task completed beyond his satisfaction, Lex had created a fleet maintenance position on the spot and offered it to him full-time. In turn, Khaleed gave Lex unswerving devotion. When Lex enrolled in a "safe families" program supplying emergency services to at-risk fosters and offered his home as a safe place for both Khaleed and Kayla, the two gave Lex love. Despite his frequently encouraging them to expand their horizons and consider opportunities elsewhere after he'd financed their way through college, both were loyal employees who would—in their words—"die for the Ryde."

"Fire me if you want, but I'mma still show up like clockwork."

Lex chuckled despite the less than pleasant sensation rolling through his stomach. Glancing at his watch he saw that Senaé's train should've come through more than an hour ago. "Let me go check on it."

Strolling towards the ticket counter, he peeped a digital marquee posting departures and arrivals. Not seeing Senaé's designated train he made an inquiry only to be informed the marquee was time sensitive and provided schedules that were most recent. Prior routes had already scrolled off and been deleted.

"But I'll be happy to find what I can for you, Mr.

Easy on My Eyes." The flirtatious counter rep levied a loaded smile while carefully typing so as not to mar the over-the-top designs on her two-inch talons. "That train was actually a few minutes early. It's already come and gone."

"Are you able to look up passengers?"

"That depends."

"On?"

"What you and I are doing when I get off."

Managing not to roll his eyes, Lex was humored at how life had changed from the days when he was ruthlessly teased for having "ink-black" skin. Thanks to the Idris Elba-Kofi Siriboe ilk, deep down dark brothers had become the business. "Ma'am...the passenger. Her name's Senaé Dawson."

"*Oh*! You're looking for a woman?" Miss Ticket Taker gained a sudden bout of professionalism. "I'm sorry, sir, but passenger information is confidential. I won't be able to help with that."

"Yeah...aiight." Shaking his head, he walked off thinking women a puzzle he'd never properly piece.

After a quick conversation with Khaleed, he dismissed his employee for the evening, opting to hang out at Union Station a while longer in case his ex appeared. An hour, several unanswered texts and voicemail messages later, he decided he'd had enough of waiting for a woman who wanted nothing to do with him.

Making his way to the Escalade, he drove to the yard, leaving the SUV in the dock to be washed and detailed the next morning. Wound up, he let the high speed of his tricked out Dodge Charger match his aggravation until he was traveling down southern California highways at well over eighty miles per hour.

Rather than kill himself or someone else, he headed for the gym to productively vent through physical exertion. Pummeling a punching bag, he chose not to brand himself a fool for thinking Senaé would ever come. Or that heaven might be willing to grant them a second chance on what used to be love.

-❀-❀-❀-

She lay pressed against the solid muscles of his broad back. Soft as fur and equally as warm, she wiggled her way to deeper comfort and contentment in a place she coveted but didn't belong. Not enticed by her panting or her pleasure, he wanted her exit.

"Get...out...my...bed."

Words slurred by sleep, his command failed to transmit with conviction or clarity. She remained in place, irking the hell out of him.

Let a female in and she'll come back until she's finished or she wins.

Fighting the heavy seduction of slumber, he tried rolling onto his back to give her the boot, but her wet tongue found his naked skin and lovingly licked, stalling an inevitable eviction.

"You...gotta...go..."

Jarred to consciousness by his ringing phone, Lex lay a moment, orienting himself before turning to find his Siberian Husky, Jazz, curled up against him in bed.

"What the?"

So much for nocturnal notions of a frisky female.

Feeling for his phone in the dark, he answered with a barely whispered, "Yeah?"

"Lex...I'm so sorry—"

"Senaé? What time is it?" Pulling the phone from his ear, he peeped the illuminated display and answered his own question. "It's 3:17 a.m. Whaddup?

Are you okay?"

"I'm fine," she assured despite obvious vocal fatigue. "I'll fill you in later. But..." She paused to yawn. "I'm here."

He pushed himself up against the headboard, his yawn mirroring hers. "Here where? Move over," he instructed his bed-hogging dog, snuggling up against him.

"Union Station. I'll take ride service to my room. I just wanted to call and let you know I made it."

Throwing back the covers, Lex eased his legs off the bed. Stretching the kinks from his back, he wearily rubbed his head. "I'm on my way."

"No, that's unnecessary. It's late. Or better stated, it's early."

"So, you want me to roll over while you find your way around L.A. at dark thirty in the morning."

"I'm not trying to disturb you...or your guest."

"What guest?"

"Whoever's posted up in your bed. Go back to sleep. I'll call you later."

Lex grunted at the terseness creeping into her tone. "Hold on a minute." Aiming his camera phone, he clicked a pic, ensuring it was time and date stamped before sending it via text. "Check that."

He waited while she did.

"What a cutie!"

"That's Jazz. She's the only female in my face."

"Sorry for assuming. I just figured you had someone significant in your life."

"And if I did, I'd invite you to California why?"

"I don't know. Maybe you made a mistake in thinking I like three-ways. Anyhow...don't drag yourself out here. I have pepper spray."

"Senaé." His tone left nothing for debate. "I haven't had a lady friend since the end of last year. So, get a coffee. Have a seat somewhere safe and I'll see you soon."

Disconnecting on her surprisingly compliant, "Yes, sir," he turned on the bedside lamp and looked at his way too comfortable canine creature. "Get your behind down. You're not even supposed to be up here."

Watching Jazz take her sweet time obeying the command, Lex patted her dog bed, reminding her where she belonged. Settling in, the black and white, blue-eyed Husky sighed dramatically before turning her back to him as if he was extra or didn't exist.

"I see how you do," he remarked, wondering if he was destined to attract attitudinal females while heading for the restroom decked solely in the glory of his birthday suit.

CHAPTER FIVE
Senaé

Really? She walked off with your charger *and* your wigs?"

Caught in the pleasure of stuffing her mouth with some of southern California's most famous chicken and waffles, Senaé merely nodded.

"You saying Grandma janked you and you let her?"

With the help of Coke Zero, Senaé swallowed the bite of unbelievably delicious breakfast. "It was only one wig, Lex. And I didn't *let* her do anything. Grandma still had some one-hundred-yard dash left in those legs. That's why you couldn't reach me. My phone was dead until I got where I could buy a charger. What?" Noting the water collecting in his light brown eyes, she sat back, arms crossed over her chest. "You know you want to laugh, Lex, so go ahead."

Her permission was all he needed to let loose belly-deep chuckles he'd obviously been keeping in check. A smile tickled her lips hearing that huge laugh she'd always loved. Rich. Intense. And full of carefree ease. It flowed across the table, its infectious energy touching her, leaving Senaé grinning broadly.

Jesus, help me 'cause this man is dangerous kinda sexy!

She fussed to keep her thoughts from dipping too far down that road. "I don't see anything funny."

"Sorry, but Gangster Granny got you, boo."

True. A long conversation that started with the

sweet-looking elder woman effusively admiring
Senaé's lavender-streaked hair segued here there and
everywhere until "Miss Mabel" was borrowing her
phone charger and telling long-winded stories about
her grandchildren. Rolling in the upper level, glass-en-
closed observation deck beneath the stars of God's
heaven, Senaé was lulled to sleep by the night sky and
Miss M.'s twisting tales. She awoke to the train rolling
away from its stop, charger gone and bareheaded.

"I'm running around looking like I was just released from prison, all cornrowed up when I glance
out the window and see Miss Mabel—if that's her real
name—walking towards the station rocking my unit."

Trotting down the stairs to the lower level, with the
train rolling Senaé couldn't do a thing except rap on a
window to get the thieving woman's attention.

"I'm standing there, hands in the air like, 'What up
with it, Miss Mabel?' She had the nerve to dangle my
charger and flip me the middle finger before walking
into the station. Oh, yeah, and she took the novel I
was reading and my black licorice. It's not funny!"

Her pathetic protest fell on deaf ears. Lex was lost
to laughter and its induced tears.

She tried withholding her own. Snorting from the
effort, she let loose until she was crying-laughing as
well.

Serves you right for trying to ditch him.

She'd lost several nights' sleep going around in
circles over whether or not to accept his generous gift.
Lovie, Ima, and Dove's badgering "encouragement"
had been relentless. But it was a feeling of restless-
ness—like she was ready for a journey of new risks—
that caused her to relent.

She accepted without expectation or false anticipation, rather with a modicum of excitement. Reshuffling appointments onto Dove's schedule and notifying clients, she'd packed and left with the ability to remotely handle the balance of her business.

Hours from her destination, she'd had a doubt attack and panicked. Disembarking at the next station with the intention of returning to Chicago, she'd simply send Lex a "thank you, but I'm sorry" text and be done with it. Inside the station, she'd made the mistake of reading a colorful advertisement mounted on a wall near the ticket counter.

You can't get where you're going if you don't go.

Simple yet powerful, it proved counsel and conviction. Arranging to board the next westbound train, Senaé sucked it up and acted like a grown woman ready for fresh experiences. Even if said experiences included her ex.

"Well, I'm glad you made it."

Sipping ice water, Senaé nodded in agreement. "I am, too."

"For the record, your cornrows look professional, not Orange is the New Black-ish."

"I can thank Dove for that."

They shared a soft smile before Lex continued. "When you didn't show, I figured you had second thoughts and decided not to come."

"I had fifth, sixth, *and* seventh thoughts, but I'm here."

"Good."

Placing her fork on her plate, she stared at the man she'd loved like tomorrow might not come, like the right here and now was all they could depend upon. He was somehow different, yet the same in comforting ways. His spirit remained that of a gentle giant.

Those light eyes still seemed able to delve into her soul, effortlessly so. The beauty of his midnight skin was more pronounced than it had been. There was a new confidence—quiet but unconcealed. The man in him was at peace and fully grown. She wanted to reach across the table to touch and taste him. "Why'd you invite me, Lex?"

"Why'd you accept?"

"Because your girl's no fool, and the cost of this vacation's on you. Honestly?" she posited when he failed to laugh. "I'm forty now and for all I know there's more life behind me than there is before me. I'm not interested in reducing the quality of my days with contention or the failure to forgive." She toyed with her napkin. "Seeing you on that stage the night of the auction I had a visceral reaction."

"It was mind-busting," he agreed when she lapsed into a temporary silence.

"I wasn't ready. Not for you or the cavalcade of emotions stampeding through. I really wanted to stop the bus and hold onto hate, but it slipped away and left me feeling some kind of softness I shouldn't. Are you going to eat that?"

Shocked by the admission that slipped through her lips, Senaé reached across the table to pilfer a chicken wing from Lex's plate, trying to avoid blurted truth. She didn't object when he blocked the action, gently laying hold of her hand in the process.

"It's alright, Naé." A shiver took its time sliding down her spine when he turned her hand over to slowly trace a line on her palm. "We both felt some things."

She'd always loved the contrast of his gold-flecked eyes against the beautiful deep of his ultra-dark skin.

His eyes were lights guiding her to the truth of the soul of the man within. Staring across that table, what she glimpsed reflected what she felt the night of the auction, and right then.

"It was probably just a lust hiccup." She down-played truth for both of their benefits. "I mean, you trigger when you run up on the dude who gave you your first orgasm," she commented, momentarily distracted by her ringing cellphone. Seeing Stanford's name on the caller I.D., she silenced it and looked up to see Lex smiling like he owned bragging rights to her best sexual releases. "What? Why're you looking smug?"

"You had to change your panties when you got home from the auction, huh?"

She snatched her hand back and managed not to laugh. "You don't know me like that."

He cocked an eyebrow and slowly rubbed a hand over his immaculate goatee. "I was your first so, actually, I do." He cleared his throat as if clearing his thoughts. "And knowing you, I know you're not one to hold onto hate. You might get hot and go off, but you always come back to truth and fairness. I don't want to misuse that...but I do ask your forgiveness."

When he reached across the table to take her hand again, she let him.

"You already know I'm straight-talking, so no of-fense meant if this doesn't come out right, but I never regretted letting you go—"

"Because?" she interrupted.

"Didn't we agree that if we ever ended we'd bless each other to leave, that there'd be no hanging on and holding each other back?"

Remembering, she nodded. They'd agreed if life

ever came to that, love would let them release each other and wish one another the best. But words and reality didn't always match.

"So, you're saying you had no remorse over us and you never missed me?" she challenged, trying to ignore the pad of his thumb stroking the back of her hand, the sensations reminding her how she used to massage him after football practice before he massaged between her legs.

"Senaé, I warned you this might not come out right." Lex sighed. "Let me say it this way. I loved you enough to want the best for you and I wasn't it back then. You deserved better. However, I've always regretted our leaving each other *the way* we did."

High school sweethearts who'd spent the night of her graduation in the minister's living room exchanging 'I Do's,' they'd started out poor with nothing except each other. Lex being drafted by the NFL changed their finances and their future in ways unimagined. Including a motorcycle accident that ended his career and their young union.

"Same here," she softly admitted. "You were injured and angry. Your career went sideways before it barely began. And I lost our…"

Twenty years later and painful truth still felt like a boulder on her tongue. The weight of the words wouldn't lift.

She smiled through sudden tears when he raised her hands to his lips and rendered what felt like gentle wings, a butterfly kiss.

"That there?" He reached across and wiped away her tears. Leaning close, he whispered, "That loss is my regret and biggest nightmare."

His admission unlocked a portal in her heart that

she'd hidden and stubbornly protected. It was a place only Lex could access. With simple sincerity he had.

Observing one other, they sat cushioned by a silence that was neither sullen nor sad. Rather, it was respectful. Reverent. It granted them a necessary moment they'd never had.

As the moment faded, Senaé sensed the heaviness that she'd carried and buried far too long being broken, lifting. The freedom of forgiving, even if not forgetting, settled sweetly in its place.

Drying residual tears with her napkin, she smiled and squeezed his hands before sitting back and eyeing his plate. "Ummm, Lex?"

"Yeah?"

"About that chicken wing. Are you going to eat it?"

"You're still greedy as all get out. Go 'head."

"Thanks." Biting into her chicken acquisition, she paused at the look on his face. "What?"

"Back in the day, Adrian claims he knew I was in love when I shared my food with you."

Wiping a napkin over her mouth, she snickered. "That's a know-it-all little brother for you. We hit each other up on social media sometimes, but I hadn't seen Adrian in a while so it was nice seeing him up on that stage at the auction. He looks like he's doing well for himself."

"He is. Did you ever remarry?"

Placing the half-eaten wing on her plate, she studied the man across from her. "Almost, but dude's wife showed at the wedding and busted that up."

"Are you serious?"

"Yep. But that's what happens when you date a man only four months. He claimed he was divorced, but I found out otherwise when we were standing at that altar exchanging those ninety-nine cent vows."

"Damn! How'd you handle that?"

She shrugged. "I took my girls on that cruise that was supposed to be a honeymoon and celebrated God's goodness in delivering me from my own ignorance. What about you, Lex? Did you ever let love back into your life?"

"Semi sort of. I had a five-year engagement that my then fiancée finally ended. According to her, I was never really all in."

She sipped her drink before asking, "Is her assessment accurate?"

"It is. Fortunately for her, she got with a solid dude who loves her like crazy. They married. Had three kids. I'm glad for her. And...before you ask, I have no biological children, but there are two young people I helped get to adulthood who might as well be mine."

Listening as he spoke on the brother-sister pair who'd happened into his life, she remembered the tenderhearted man he'd always been and considered his actions divine. "I'm glad you have that. If I'm being intrusive, I apologize...but were you ever able to reconnect with your mother or brothers?"

Seeing a shadow of pain pass over his features, she regretted questioning, despite his forthright answer.

"I've spent a grip looking for my three youngest brothers, but they're lost in the wind." He assumed they'd been adopted and their last names changed, or they'd been lost in or never entered the foster care system. Relatives back home in Mississippi were clueless on the matter. "I did, however, find the brother who's a year younger than me."

"Really?" She smiled at the pleasure lifting his full, luscious lips in an easy grin.

"We reconnected twelve years ago. He's in Denver with a good wife and one son. And my mother's there. In a mental institution."

She reached over and rubbed his arm, feeling solid muscle beneath his sleeve. "I'm so sorry."

"Don't be. I visit every time I can. Sometimes she knows me, sometimes she thinks I'm Dad. But, she's alive and I'm good with that. Back to you: were you... ever blessed...with children?"

Her response was slow in coming. "Two godsons. But, like you, none of my own," she nearly whispered. Suppressing the sudden emotions threatening to clog her throat, she asked in a hurry, "Do you miss football?"

Those broad shoulders shrugged. "Not really. I wasn't interested in sidelining, so I let the walk-away be complete without trying my hand at commentary. I did, however, coach pee-wee leagues a quick minute and enjoyed it."

"Do you think you'll ever try love again?" Her blurting had her feeling as if she had Tourette's.

His reaching across the table and slowly wiping a crumb from the corner of her mouth startled her, as much as his answer did.

"I'm already open."

The lullaby of the Pacific Ocean a soothing serenade on repeat, she slept like a well-fed baby—dreamless, without worries. She'd managed to briefly admire the exquisite accommodations offered by the Black-owned Bed and Breakfast before showering and falling into the seductive softness of her queen-size bed. On a stomach content with chicken and waffles she slept until the need to use the restroom pulled her back to consciousness.

"God, I feel drunk from tiredness," she muttered, finished with her business and crawling beneath the covers and back into the arms of slumber. When her cellphone chimed within minutes, she answered without hesitation. Lex said he'd check in. "Hi."

Her voice was an unintentional purr.

"Hello to you, too, Senaé. And what's wrong with you?"

Shoot! Smart phones have caller I.D. for a good reason. Use it!

Having let his last six calls roll to voicemail, Stanford Browning was not high on her "I Want to Talk to" list. And for the first time, she considered the fact that she'd never assigned him his own distinguishing ring tone. That alone should've let her know he wasn't man-for-life material. "Nothing's wrong. Why?"

"You sound like you're either thinking about or just had sex. Which I hope you haven't."

"That'll never be your business."

"It always is, Senaé, but apparently you don't understand this." He barged on before she could counter that foolishness. "Seeing as how you didn't bother to confirm, I'll trust you safely arrived wherever it is you went."

Really, Jesus? I'm fully disinterested in this man's ish.

She refused to bite back at the caller with his fake New England accent. "Yes, Stanford, I did."

"Did what? Arrived safely, or had sex? Never mind, Senaé, I don't need to know right this minute. You can, however, tell me where the hell you are to prevent me from resorting to behaving like some lowlife stalker and making use of some god-awful friend-finding app."

"My whereabouts aren't your concern, Stanford, but do what you want. You're a grown man."

Opting for speaker mode, she placed the phone atop a plethora of pillows and burrowed deeper in bed. Within seconds, she was lightly snoring.

"Senaé!"

"Huh?"

"So this is what we've come to—you somewhere in the world and me sitting in Chicago wondering who you're screwing, and when you're coming home again?"

Wanting nothing more than to slip back into sleep, she exhaled noisily. "No, Stan." She intentionally used the derivative of his name, knowing he detested it. "You have that twisted. I never gave you cause to worry who I was with. That creeping category was solely yours." She'd pumped the brakes after learning he'd been with three other women during their brief, lackluster relationship. "And what we've come to is nothing. If you missed the memo, we're completely done. *Finit.* All this gum-bumping is simply you missing the water now that the well's run dry."

Stanford Browning's sighing on the opposite end felt melodramatic, in keeping with his local, on-air persona and the wannabe actor in him. "I think it's best we wait for you to return before discussing the nature of our relationship."

"I think it's best you stop acting like a brain injury survivor with a memory deficit."

"Listen, I owned up to my actions when you confronted me with them. I never lied."

"Gold badge time."

"Don't be snarky, Senaé. We deserve a second

chance."

"You 'deserve' nothing more than friendship. *If* that."

"With benefits?"

Lord, I wish this man would put his head in the oven with the gas on full blast.

"Are you in-between women?" It was the only logical reason for his crawling back as if she was a fill-in fit to be his ideal woman.

"That's not important, Senaé. The more pressing issue to answer is did you, or do you, love me?"

She answered truthfully. "No."

"Right! My thoughts towards you precisely. I mean, I caught occasional feelings, but they weren't deep or abiding. And there's nothing wrong with that. We weren't in love. We just had good sex. So, let's pick up where we left off and enjoy what we had. My being with other women shouldn't bother you."

"It doesn't. Now, stop with the incessant calling and texting. It's not a good look. If I want to reach you, I know how to," she informed before disconnecting. "You fast-ejaculating fool." Easily she drifted back to the edge of sleep, finishing her thought before completely succumbing.

And the only one of us who had good sex was you.

The sand beneath her bare feet was wonderfully rough, cool. She wiggled her toes deeper beneath the grains, and sighed in appreciation of rolling, crashing ocean waves.

Lord, this is good. Thank You.

She'd claimed and maintained her seat on the beach since waking and showering. Supplied with endless Arnold Palmers and trays of deliciousness she felt she'd been granted a little heaven on earth. More than drinks or appetizers, Senaé relished the gift of tranquility.

Eyes shielded by Lex's sunshades that she had yet to return, she lifted her feet and leaned back against the recliner, seduced by the soft, Santa Monica breeze.

"I didn't realize I was so tired."

She was a woman who put her whole self into whatever she did. Her work as a licensed aesthetician and makeup artist came from the heart. Heightening the beauty of women was her ministry, and her blog was her baby. Passion and dedication didn't exempt her from exhaustion. It added to it. It wasn't until she stopped the proverbial train and got off that she felt the jagged edges of her weariness.

"And now I'm here and I intend to enjoy this peace and paradise."

Just as soon as she forwarded the amended beauty ambassador contract. Product development was already completed; this amended agreement simply offered the option of extending her road tour. With her Queen of Shades blog and social media platforms having subscribers in the millions, the offer made sense on the part of the parent company. She came with a ready-made customer base. Her subscribers trusted her opinion and product recommendations. Now, a long-held dream of her own quality products for specific needs of deeper hued women had manifested.

Her iPad open, she scanned the agreement she'd read, reread and consulted her attorney over. It was solid with advantages including having a say in packaging, as well as her likeness being utilized in promotional advertisements. Her role as beauty ambassador for her own products would involve multi-city meet-ups. She was thrilled by the prospect of seeing in person many of the women who'd made her platform a success, and having the opportunity to thank them. The sole drawback was having to farm out existing makeover appointments. She loved her clientele and didn't relish the idea of disappointing them, but this opportunity was an answered prayer she couldn't decline.

"Here's to newness."

Raising her ice tea-lemonade cocktail, she toast-ed heaven and tossed a hand up in purest praise. A home-owning business woman with good health and loving, supportive friends, she was undoubtedly bless-ed. Only a strong and steady love life was nonexistent.

In no hurry, yet open to it when it arrived, she told herself good love took time. She was forty and de-served better than booty calls. "When I'm ready, love will happen."

Opening the newest installment in the Easy Raw-lins series, she turned to the page she'd left off on only for her cell phone to ring. Seeing the caller identified, her smile was sweet. "Hello, Lex."

"Hey, BoBo. You still rocking a wig, or did a seagull snatch it?"

"You have jokes, Mr. Comedian," she replied with a laugh, amazed at her lack of embarrassment in having allowed Lex to see her all cornrowed up and wigless. He hadn't batted an eyelash, whereas Stan-ford—who was all too quick to hint her wig-wearing bordered on ridiculous—would have been mortified. Dove was a master "braidologist," as she called herself, and her designs were flawless and worthy of being showcased without a covering. Senaé simply loved the flexibility wigs afforded, allowing her to change color, length, style and even texture to achieve whatever look she wanted depending on her attire, the occasion, or her mood. "I'll have you know I'm sitting on the beach baldheaded. I shaved it all off this morning."

"Okay, Milkdud. I can get with that."

"Are you for serious?"

"'Ey, do what you do. Your natural hair's on hit."

She sat a moment remembering how he'd always encouraged Senaé to be Senaé, without the need for false airs or artifice. "Thanks…and I was only kidding. I didn't shave my head. I'm still rocking my inmate number two-oh-five-eight braids."

His deep chuckle triggered those belly flutters she seemed prone to in his presence. "Sounds good. I'm not too far, and should be there in ten."

"Oh Lord, Lex!" Assessing the shorts and tank top she wore, she admitted to being improperly dressed for the dinner for which he'd made reservations. "I've been so busy being lazy and chilling on this beach that I lost track of time. The time zone difference and the fact that I didn't get out of bed until after two, has my inner clock off."

"You must need the rest."

"I do." She didn't miss his momentary pause or the sliver of disappointment in his voice when he spoke again.

"How about you go ahead and chill tonight. Our dinner date can wait 'til tomorrow."

"No, it can't! I'm starving. And you know how I get when I'm hangry."

"Hungry and angry, huh? What're you angry about?"

"Nothing yet, but leave me sitting here hungry and see what happens. Mind if I make a suggestion?"

"No, ma'am."

"Can we order take-out and eat here on the beach?"

"We can. Have a taste for anything?"

"Yes. You."

Girl, what the heazy? Have you lost the teaspoon of good sense God gave you?

Hitting herself in the head with her paperback novel, she opened her mouth to apologize. "Lex—"

"I see you still can't tame that tongue."

The humor in his voice allowed her to relax. "I'm going to blame that blurt on sitting too long in the sun. I'll take my favorite, if you don't mind—"

"Chinese food it is. We'll discuss that other when I get there. See you soon."

"See you." She disconnected before her mouth could make more of a mess. "Naé, I swear you have issues." Namely, six months' worth of unintended abstinence.

After her split with Stanford, she'd needed a break from mess and men. She'd spent the past months refocusing her energies on bettering herself and her career. She was proud of her professional and personal accomplishments, particularly joining a gym.

"Now, if I actually went, I might lose these extra twenty-plus pounds hanging around hounding me like a broke relative."

Snickering, she slid her sandals on her feet and collected her belongings before heading across the uneven sand, repeatedly pulling on her shorts in a losing effort to keep them from riding up high thanks to the expanded junk in her trunk and the thickness of her solid-rock thighs.

❖─❖─❖

I'm here.

His text came through just as she was changing into something appropriate for a sexy guest she wanted to avoid getting busy with. The off-the-shoulder maxi-length dress with bold, turquoise and tan asymmetrical stripes kissed her curves without overly advertising. Slipping her feet into four-inch wedge sandals, she grabbed his sunglasses and headed for the lobby of the Bed and Breakfast—hungry, but happy.

Exchanging hellos with the front desk attendant, she reached for the front door only to pause at the particularly disturbing sound of an engine revving.

Hearing Lex's voice above the soul-jarring noise, she wanted to turn and run in the opposite direction. Instead, she slowly moved like a woman compelled by forces beyond herself.

Exiting the lobby, she found Lex in deep conversation with the man she recognized as co-owner of the establishment. Their conversation was of no consequence. She could only see Lex.

Viewing him seated astride a monster of a motorcycle, loudly revving its engine, Senaé was suddenly eighteen again.

Just like that, it all came back. The horror. The pain. The trauma of one of the greatest losses of her life. When he removed the helmet from his head and looked in her direction, she knew he'd correctly interpreted the dismay fanned across her face. A hand on her stomach, she was suddenly helpless to emotions swirling like a hurricane. Feeling violently sick, she turned and hurried away as he lowered the Harley's kickstand, calling her name.

Only the height of her heels kept her from flat out

running, unfortunately allowing him to catch up with her in the lobby.

"Senaé—"

She whirled on him. *"Is that yours?"*

"No, I was testing—"

"How could you, Lex? Why would you?"

Unconscious of the tears streaming down her face, she jerked away from his offered embrace.

"Naé, I apologize."

"Keep your damn apologies! Right now, they mean zero to me."

"Can you let me explain?"

"What the hell kind of explanation could you possibly give? Are you ass-out ignorant or just insensitive?"

"Damn, woman, I'm neither and you know this!"

"Then why roll up on a demon cycle thing when it's responsible for killing our baby?"

CHAPTER SIX
Lex

He was established. Seven-figures kind of financially sound and solvent. Forty-two, over six feet of granite-like muscle, yet he felt helpless and inept. Watching her sling clothing into her suitcase, he was whisked backwards to being that young, busted up football player all over again.

❈ ❈ ❈

"Come on, BoBo, you can't be on that."

"You don't think I'd look sexy up there?" Suited and booted in black leather pants, she'd slowly turned, modeling her kryptonite curves for his benefit.

"Hell, yeah. But you have no business riding."

"*Please*, Lexie Lex. Just one slow roll around the block, baby, and I promise that's it." She'd batted those lashes and slowly licked his earlobe, whispering that when they finished, she'd take her time riding him.

The thought of being buried deep inside his wife with her on top, her moans and pleasure leading them, he'd erred against his sane judgment. "Five minutes, and we're done. And you better ride me right."

"You already know I will."

Playfully swatting her round behind, he'd climbed onto the hog he was contemplating buying before helping her mount. Handing her the one and only helmet, he waited while she fastened it before revving up with one last reminder it was only once around the block. "Hold on."

Arms clenched about his waist, his slow acceleration resulted in her demanding speed. She wanted to feel the wind. He indulged her a tiny bit, enticed by her bold nature—an aspect he loved most about her essence. That and the fearless fight she'd demonstrated on his behalf when he'd first transferred to the high school she attended.

"Tarlon, I know you ain't talking about nobody being stupid!" She'd gone up against a six-foot-five-inch basketball star and class bully for him. "You might wanna ask Lex to tutor you in math so you can learn to count by twos."

He hadn't needed her intervention, but the class erupting in hoots and howls had diverted attention away from his struggling to read a simple sentence. All because of his father's death.

Her husband murdered by police for resisting arrest in a case of mistaken identity, his mother's periodic bouts of deep depression tragically bloomed into full blown mental illness. In his father's absence, their family became nomadic. Unemployed and drifting from relative to relative, house to house, and state to state, his mother left one of her five children behind with each relocation until all five had been parceled out in someone else's care like kittens. Winding up with Mama Peaches at the age of eleven gave him desperately needed stability, but by then his education had already suffered the consequences of transient living and he was behind in his studies. Despite an elevated aptitude for all things numerical, he struggled academically. Particularly with language arts. Reading, writing, comprehension: they were all hassles that left him highly embarrassed and frustrated. Until Senaé.

With his mother's abandonment and Senaé's own stepfather trauma, they instantly bonded. When others mislabeled Senaé as attitudinal and prone to popping off, he saw the truth: her guarded defensiveness was simply self-preservation resulting from pain. She'd been unceremoniously rejected from her mother's home and sent to live with her grandmother based on something over which she had no control: her skin. Rather than running away from the depth of her complexion and choosing a lighter love able to "elevate her status," she fell for Lex whose "midnight velvet" complexion was even deeper than hers. Crazy loyal, she became his boo and refused to let him concede academic defeat. Weeks into their relationship, Senaé was on his case to address his challenge.

"Go to the school counselor, Lex, like Mama Peaches said. Maybe they can help."

"I don't need help when I got the NFL scouting me." A football Phenom, he broke records and exceeded athletically.

"But you need to understand that contract before signing."

Several months into dating, Senaé constantly encouraged even while helping him to the best of her ability. It wasn't until she threatened to terminate their relationship if he didn't do something more proactive that he cooperated. That's how, three months before his high school graduation, he learned he was dyslexic. When she stood by him, sitting outside the tutor's office doing her homework while he received aid and learned necessary skills, Lex was convinced she was ride-or-die—the kind of woman he'd one day make his wife. Learning she was pregnant a week before her own graduation, he did, vowing to give her love for life. Hers was a passion and affection he couldn't deny. But he should have learned to deny her versus giving into her wants and whims. Had he followed his own misgivings about her being three-and-a-half months pregnant on the back of a Harley, he wouldn't have shattered his right leg, and impaired the sight in his left eye. His pro-ball career wouldn't have been lost. Their marriage might've survived. And, most importantly, their child would be alive.

⬧⬧⬧

"Senaé..."

"Move, Lex." Luggage beneath one arm, oversized tote bag hanging from the other, she unsuccessfully tried to maneuver around him as he blocked her path. "I won't ask you again."

"Neither of us is moving, Senaé, until we say what needs to be said."

"Oh, you want to talk now? Fine!" She flung the items she held onto a nearby sofa, her tension and tone escalating. "Start by explaining why you'd even bring that thing around me when you know I hate it!"

"Do you really think I'd deliberately hurt you that way?"

"I obviously don't know you or what you'd do!"

Inhaling deeply, he kept his voice as level as he could. "The motorcycle's not mine, Senaé. It belongs to the owners of this place. I didn't bring it here like some perverted prank."

"But you want it? Right?"

"I do. And so you know, I have others—"

"*Why?*"

"I've never been no one's punk." He jabbed a finger towards the door as if the motorcycle was parked in their presence. *"It was either get back on that thing or let it conquer me!"*

The roar of his voice shook them both, leaving them in a sludge of silence.

His eyes closed as he slowly breathed his way through an emotional avalanche.

"I blame myself. No one else." His voice was quiet but strangled. "I never should've let you on that hog. I had no business taking you around the block. That was my doing, and I live with that on a daily."

A tense stillness ensued that was only broken by the gentleness of her touch that proved an electrical shock. Opening his eyes, he found her looking up at him, tears streaming, face filled with unexpected tenderness.

"You're not God, Lex. You had no way of knowing that drunk idiot would run a red light and smash into us."

"No, but," he hammered his chest with an open palm, "a man's supposed to take care of, not kill, what he loves."

"Lex, we're still here so don't—"

"Yeah, Senaé, we're here! Divorced. All kind of split up, so let the truth be what it be. I. Killed. Us!" Chest heaving, he sat on the sofa arm, head in hand, bombarded by memories. Memories of weeks in the hospital, rehabilitation and occupational therapy, dealing with visual impairment, and learning to walk again. A rookie recruit with a dire prognosis, he'd lost his NFL contract and the newly improved lifestyle they'd barely begun to live.

"I own that I made matters more difficult then they should've been." Bitter and brooding, he'd turned their occasional, recreational use of marijuana into his daily way of coping with physical pain and trauma. But weed and the hard liquor he took to drinking couldn't curtail his escalating anger over his lost career. Yet, it was the loss of their child, the physical and emotional pain it produced in her, and his inability to balance tragedies and comfort her in the face of his own physical injuries that destroyed him. "So…" He focused light brown eyes on the face of a woman he'd—to the best of youthful ability—loved more than breathing. "That's why I don't regret letting you go. I was wilding out, and didn't deserve you. After all I put you through, the only thing I deserved was the punishment of not having you. So, I took it."

"Like a man? In unnecessary silence?" Her exhalation was soft with sorrow. "Lex, I agreed to end our marriage because you withdrew into yourself and evicted me emotionally when we were both hurting." Her stepping to him and placing a gentle palm against his face while saying, "But, honey, I never blamed you for what happened to our baby," broke the chains of guilt that had long held him in bondage.

Still seated on the arm of the sofa, he felt her arms wind about him, permitting him to lean into the strength of a compassionate woman. Her repeated whispers, "It's okay," were swallowed beneath the raw sounds of his regret. Her body shaking with the purging of grief right along with his, Lex embraced his ex in a relentless grip. Together, they clung to each other and let healing flow to its content.

The colors of day caressed the sky's canvas as the sun began its majestic descent into the welcoming arms of a laughing, frolicking Pacific Ocean. Seated on sand, hands clasped, they were soothed by nature's display. They were without words. Their spirits had already spoken a language fully understood and solely comprised of tears.

Feeling a wholeness he hadn't experienced in eons, he squeezed her hand and kissed the top of her head. "Two dollars for your thoughts."

Her laugh was soft. "That your way of saying I'm expensive and high maintenance?"

"Naw, BoBo, it's called inflation."

"Why'd you give me that crazy nickname?" His quiet chuckle caused her to look up at him. "Come on, Lex, you never would tell me."

Rubbing his goatee, he studied ocean waves while responding. "Back in the day you were this skinny, scrawny thing except when it came to breasts and booty. I was like, 'Well, damn, she's all arched out like somebody took a bow and stretched it.' Bow times two, for the top and the bottom, equals BoBo. Get it?"

After staring at him a moment, she sucked her teeth and repositioned her head against his shoulder. "That doesn't even make sense."

"Yeah, well, you answered to it."

The consequent silence was comfortable, intimate until Senaé breached it. "I didn't realize I was still so stuck in parts of our loss until..." She paused to exhale and swallow. "When I saw you sitting on that cycle, it was like being swept up by a flood that I couldn't fight. Call it crazy, but it was as if I was helpless to losing you...us...miscarrying our baby. *Again*."

"Trust. I get it," he reassured, releasing her hand to wrap his arm about her. "It's called overdue mourning."

"That's one thing I let myself do, Lex. I shut down

on God. Screamed. Cussed. Threw things. So, believe me. I grieved."

"Yeah, baby, but not with me." He leaned back as her head snapped up as if she'd been hit with revelation.

Her words were slow in coming. "You're right. You went one way, I went the other, and we never truly grieved together."

"Until today. Let me get this." The incoming call he accepted was brief, lasting less than a minute. "For sure, Kayla. Thanks for being on it." Disconnecting, he got to his feet and extended a hand so she could do the same. He pulled her close. "Earlier…after what happened…I made a call and had a gift delivered. It just arrived."

"And it is…?"

"Something I think we could benefit from. Trust me on it," he requested, kissing her forehead. "And just so you know, Kayla—the person who called—is my administrative assistant."

"Lex, your life is your life, just like mine is mine. You don't owe me an explanation."

"Maybe not, but I was one-hundred when I said I haven't had a lady friend in a minute." He felt himself warming when she removed one of her hands from his and placed gentle fingers on the back of his head.

"That makes two of us."

"Oh, you swinging both ways these days?"

Her laughter was quiet but bright. "You still have subzero sense. I haven't had a *man* friend in a while. Do you want one?"

"*Another dude?* Hell to the naw times two!"

"Oh my gosh, stop clowning! I'm referring to a lady friend, Lex."

"No, baby, I don't want a female friend." He withheld a moan when her fingers slid to the base of his neck and massaged in a slow, circular pattern.

"What do you want?"

"A woman. *My woman.*"

Easing an arm about her waist, he took his time in the incline, allowing her the opportunity to avoid his kiss if she was disinterested. Instead, reciprocating his want, she elevated on her tiptoes until their lips met.

Mmm-hmm...this right here.

His mouth moving sweetly over hers, he acknowledged the hungry sensations barreling up from his feet only to flash like fire in the center of his soul, his body. Thirsty, he delved deeper until feeling drugged, tipsy.

"Uhh...yeah...yo, excuse me...but I'm looking for a Mr. Ryde."

Disengaging was a torture he didn't appreciate. Feeling evil-eyed, he peeped the youngster standing several feet away. Recognizing the company name on the side of the box he held, Lex backed down on his annoyance and accepted the delivery, tipping the driver generously.

"Is that my gift?"

Grinning at the excitement in her tone, he shifted the box behind his back. "Actually, it's ours, but you owe me payment. Give it up, lips."

Her grabbing the waistband of his jeans and pulling him in, slipping her tongue into his mouth and doing what she did until they were both moaning, had him staggering.

"Well, alright...paid in full," he jested when she released him. Loving the brightness of her smile, he was suddenly serious. "It'll be dark soon." Managing the box in one hand, he removed the string securing it and opened the lid with the other. "It may not be easy, but I'm of the opinion we should do this."

He watched her peek at the contents before lifting a quizzical eyebrow at him. He simply nodded, encouraging her to remove a decorative jar of pink and blue sand swirled in a visually stunning pattern.

"It's lovely, Lex, but what's the significance?"

Placing the box on the beach, he cradled her hands so that they held the jar together. "It represents our son...or daughter."

"I wish we would've found out the sex instead of waiting for the birth the way I wanted."

"Like you told me, there was no way you could've predicted what went down." Seeing tears welling in her eyes, he rested his forehead against hers. "We weren't perfect, BoBo. We were parents. If only for a moment. Can we honor him or her together and say 'goodbye'?"

With the sun dipping and the sky a deepening palette, Lex lead a prayer that honored the Creator, his words like a comforting cradle for the child their arms had never held. As their unified 'Amen' floated on the breeze, they stood at the shore, opened the jar of sand and prepared for release.

Quietly, he invited, "Anything you want to say?" He anchored her against his side as she struggled through her tears, her voice flowing in a small whisper.

"We love you, sweet one."

Nodding in agreement, he echoed the sentiment. "Rest well. Ready, baby?"

"No...but it's necessary."

His hands anchoring hers, together they tilted the jar, reverently pouring sparkling grains of colored sand near the water's edge. Two decades of heaviness lifting, they watched ocean waves receive that which was symbolic and freeing. When she turned, sobbing against the wide wall of his chest, Lex held his first and only love, giving her his strength as their mutual sorrow was absorbed by God's incredible grace.

CHAPTER SEVEN
Senaé

She awoke the next morning disoriented, but truly peaceful and content. Feeling rock-solid, sexy pressure against her behind, she understood the cause of her confusion. After six months of abstinence sharing intimate space felt foreign. More importantly, she'd slept with a man.

Resituating herself onto her side, she stared at heaven's sweetest specimen, wishing they'd done more than simply slept.

God, help me if I'm crazy, but I want this man.

Despite their painful past. Because of his consideration and care. His quiet power and sexy strength.

A ceremonious farewell at sunset had proven a God-sent gift, cathartic. Not only was it a bridge paving a departure from grief and a path to deeper forgiveness, she'd been greatly moved by the sheer thoughtfulness. His evident kindness allowed her to strip away layers of angst and give name to something long misinterpreted. Mixed within her "overdue mourning" was a sentiment long avoided: disappointment. In herself. In Lex. For being torn apart and leaving each other when at their worst, for failing to have each other's backs in tragedy.

"We *were* young and dumb," she softly concurred, outlining his eyebrow with a fingertip.

She halted the motion when he made a sound deep in his throat before mumbling something incoherent.

"You still talk in your sleep."

She smiled, appreciative of the ways in which he hadn't changed even while enticed by the newness of him. Inhaling the clean scent of his cologne, she slowly eased against his body, feeling his solid length and strength through the jeans he'd slept him.

Loving the fact that he was still prone to morning erections, her lips lifted in a wicked grin.

I'mma 'bout to wake baby boy up so we can handle this grown and sexy business!

Her thoughts were interrupted by the chime of an incoming text.

By now you should've had some of that thick, rich Mandika warrior stick. If not, we're no longer friends.

Snickering quietly, she answered Dove's text, advising her to refrain from grown folks' business.

Immediately the phone rang. She smiled, hearing her friend.

"Your sad response lets me know you haven't. So, either get some, Naé, or I'm canceling your godmother status."

Not wanting to awaken Lex, she resorted to whispering. "Honey, that's for life. Now, what do you want?"

"Why're you whispering? Are you in bed with Lex?"

"Dove, you're about to hear a disconnect."

"Oooo, you are! I'm so proud of you, you nasty harlot."

"Bye, Your Foolishness."

"No, for real, Naé, wait! Your stupid Stanford just

left the salon."

"What?"

"Yes, huntee, and that makes twice since you hopped that train to Cali. He was in here talking about you two getting back together and trying to get the 4-1-1 on you and your whereabouts."

"What did you tell him?"

"To eat rocks."

She snorted back a laugh. "Good. I hope he enjoys them."

"His dumb self probably would. But on a serious note, Naé, dude's always been strange, but he seems to be wilding out on something."

"Like drugs?"

"No...more like he's not clicking mentally. Go online and check yesterday's article on him in the paper. Some woman accused him of touching her inappropriately at a company event. Dude's response was denying he was even present at the time. And the pic they posted? He's all bugged-eyed and smiling like he won a trip to Disneyland. Girl, I need you to put his ass on mute and stay safe 'cause his wheels don't roll right."

Stretching and yawning, she acknowledged Dove's observations. Stanford's uptight, persnickety penchants had contributed to their breakup. He was quirky, particular, and intense with a bad habit of minimizing and trivializing how his actions negatively impacted others.

"No worries, Dove, I blocked him last night," she whispered. And she had. Spending the evening with Lex, she'd ignored Stanford's calls which merely resulted in an absurd amount of texts that seemed oddly pleading, desperate. Annoyed to hell, she'd blocked his contact as well as his email address. "He knows we went our separate ways, but I had to reinforce that and revoke his access."

"Good for you. Now, get off the phone and go get yourself an orgasm. Love you. Bye."

Smiling, she placed her phone on the nightstand and turned onto her side, watching a sleeping Lex.

This is a good man.

Mentally and emotionally exhausted by shared grief and goodbyes, last night they'd returned to her room, ordered Chinese, and—with the ocean air turning chilly—sat on the floor in front of a lit fire eating. Talking. Sharing. Filling in the chapters of their lives, cloaked by an intense intimacy that defied absence.

There were hilarious recounts of life's events, as well as sobering moments such as Lex undergoing multiple surgeries in an effort to right the visual impairment resulting from that long ago motorcycle accident. Thankfully, he'd recovered eight-five-percent visibility in his left eye, but his perpetual use of sunglasses resulted from light sensitivity, not some effort at cool-sexy. Hours passed unnoticed as they indulged in the activity of learning the other's adult self. The more they learned the more it was confirmed: the one they'd initially fell in love with still existed.

Taking advantage of his state of sleep, she stroked his eyebrow, studying him affectionately.

Rejected by a color-conscious stepfather, she'd been shipped from New York to Chicago—broken-hearted and hard. But the day the newly transferred Lexington Ryde entered gym class, her feelings were on and popping. She softened. He was two years older, quiet, and serious. Despite years in Chicago, he still had a hint of "southern boy" about him. Unique, she fell hard in her feelings, and a lust that left them mutually surrendering their virginity.

Two decades later and we're still managing some seriously hot, sexual hunger.

It was undeniably present, potent. Yet, at his insistence, they agreed that last night was dedicated to reconnecting on an emotional and spiritual level. Far from easy, they refrained from getting naked and taking care of grown folks' needs. That didn't prevent gentle, explorative touches. On a makeshift bed of multiple blankets and a mound of pillows before the fireplace, they whispered confidences in between toying and teasing one another until dangerously stimulated.

Back in the day, we would've been so butt-naked-busy that our old dusty, musty, six-cat-having landlord would've been beating on the ceiling of our basement apartment hollering for us to "shut that sh*t up".

Stifling a laugh, she grudgingly conceded there was value in restraint. Waiting was its own aphrodisiac.

I'm headed home tomorrow, Mr. Lex. You have until tonight to fill me up with this here good chocolate.

Rolling away from him, she pushed the covers back, intent on the restroom. His arm landing about her waist prevented her exodus.

"Where you going?"

Allowing him to pull her back, she turned and greeted him with a sweet and simple kiss. "To handle nature's call."

"Baby, I got much nature in need of your handling. How 'bout you call on that?" he sexily suggested, positioning them both, pelvis to pelvis.

A deep purr escaped her lips, encountering the

solid evidence of what she'd missed these past twenty years. "Well, good morning, Your Thickness."

"Morning to you, too, Queen of my Dreams."

"Am I really?" She squirmed as he nuzzled her throat, his lips and tongue warm velvet against her skin.

"Always was. Always will be."

That is so sweet were the words that filtered through her mind but never left her mouth with his hand sliding beneath her pajama top creating a sensual distraction. She felt treasured, yet tortured, by his slow, gentle skimming of her waist, her torso, and hips—clearly demonstrating through the intensity of touch that reorienting himself with her physique was the only matter of importance to him. When his hand eased down her back and beneath the waistband of her pajama bottoms she shivered at the delicious, nerve-tingling contact.

Kneading the roundness of her high behind, his massive grip was possessive. "What?" she barely breathed, when he emitted a guttural groan.

"*Damn, baby!* I've missed this astronomical ass."

"Oh, hush!" She pushed him away with a laugh and left their makeshift bed. "I'm taking a shower."

"When you finish, let's head to my place so I can do the same. Better yet… About that shower stall. Is it big enough for a man and a woman?"

She looked back at him. "It is. *But,*" she added when he moved as if to join her. "We're not showering together, Lex."

"Not yet," he countered, falling back on a mound of pillows, arms propped behind his head, grinning like he knew something she didn't. "But watch. We will."

Warmed by his sultry promise, she suddenly wanted him to make good on it. She wanted him to the point that her feminine places ached. But she also had a crazy need to exercise self-control she'd never exhibited in their past, to prove that she was good and grown versus some sex-starved teen harassed by hormones. She was fabulously forty and knew who and what she wanted. Unquestionably, that was Lex. She would take him to bed to experience him in ways she hadn't. But in her time and not before. She was the queen in control.

I want this man like damn! *But I need more than lust. I need love.*

Dealing with men like Stanford Browning, she'd hidden that need somewhere deep. One day with Lex and it had resurrected.

"'Ey, BoBo, let me use the restroom before you post up in it."

Pausing in the doorway, she moved aside to let him enter. Instead, he stood towering over her, stroking her with a torrid look loaded with heat and tenderness. As if on auto pilot, her fingers strayed to the muscles exposed by the A-shirt he'd slept in. Slowly, she stroked his biceps, his chest. His strength had always been her weakness. When he slid a hand to her back and pulled her close she lifted on her toes, treating her mouth to his.

God, this man can kiss.

Back in the day, they'd been equals. Giving each other their virginity, they'd learned sex and lovemaking. But kissing this Lex was kissing a truly experienced man with sensual tricks up his sleeve. The slow and controlled way he licked her lips and tasted her tongue hinted he had plenty treasures for her pleasure on hold.

Heating easily, she leaned back with a hand at his chest. "I'm stopping this."

"Scared we'll wind up in that shower?"

"Possibly, and right now you owe me. I won that birthday bid and I want my date all day. Starting with breakfast. As in waffles, pecan pancakes, biscuits and gravy. Country ham. Sausage. Cheese grits. Sugar rice. Oven-roasted potatoes. Cran-Apple juice. A caramel macchiato with extra whipped cream. And scrambled egg whites since I'm eating light."

"Alright, Your Greediness. Let me handle my business," he suggested, entering the bathroom with that sexy, deep laugh.

"Lex?"

"Yeah, baby?"

"I love your kisses now as much as I did back when, but let that mouthwash hit that morning breath."

Slapping his firm behind, she jumped out of reach and slammed the door, laughing like a woman cherished.

She fell in love with Jazz, his fluffy, blue-eyed Husky, and might've stayed playing with her half the day while Lex showered and dressed if it weren't for her stomach growling and grumbling. Leaving Jazz with a promise to see her again, Senaé held the hand Lex offered as he led her to the garage.

"Your home is gorgeous, Lex." She felt pure joy that he'd achieved success as a self-made man. He lived well in a home displaying elegant simplicity with a masculine spin. Neither ostentatious nor in your face, his beachfront single-story "cottage" (as he called it) was spacious and well-appointed, reflecting the fact that he could afford what he wanted.

"Thanks, but Kayla gets the credit. She made me have it professionally decorated. Left to me, we'd probably be sitting on pleather and plastic."

"So your good taste is limited to cars," she teased as he held open the passenger door of his Mercedes-AMG Roadster. Sitting in luxury, she added, "And women?"

"Cars? I agree. But that woman thing? I'mma need a little convincing."

Pleasurable jolts raced through her body when he leaned in and slowly trailed his tongue down her neck. His full and luscious lips, warm and talented, most definitely had her six-month celibate body on burn.

You will be led by your head, not your hoochie or your coochie.

His mouth below her ear, she whispered in his, "Convinced?"

Positioning himself so they were face-to-face, she shivered when he stroked a lazy finger from her chin to her chest. "For now, but I'mma need to taste some other things."

Lawd, I'mma need to change my panties.

Determined not to be the only one affected by sexual play, she slid a hand into the front pocket of his jeans and slowly felt around as if in search of something.

"You're in dangerous territory." His raspy tones and the sudden hardness in his pocket were evidence of her effect.

"I'm simply getting your keys so I can drive this puppy."

"You wanna drive? Or you wanna ride?"

"You or this AMG?"

"Both."

"Most definitely."

Her eyebrow arched as he reached for her waist. His turning her body to face him, squatting, and placing her leg over his shoulder caused her eyes to grow big. Pushing up the hem of her high-low dress, he followed its trajectory, his tongue traveling a course over her smooth skin with gentle licks and nips that left her breathless. Leaning her slightly backward when he reached the apex of her thighs, he blew a warm, steady breath against her lace-covered paradise.

She waited. She wanted. Heart pounding with pleasure, she looked expectantly at him. "Lex…"

He licked her lace, causing her hips to grind against the seat, instantly in need of relief.

She was stimulated and irritated when he backed away.

Righting her skirt, he stood and handed her the seatbelt. "Strap up, baby."

"You're serious? That's all I get?"

"You played in my pocket? I'mma let you percolate."

"I can't stand you." Crossing arms over her breasts, she flounced back against the seat as his lush lips spread in a lusty, playful grin. "Don't smile at me."

Chuckling softly, he closed her door after declaring, "Breakfast first. You're dessert."

Fingers intertwined, they made the drive from Santa Monica to Catalina, old school R&B bumping through the sound system. The air between them was loaded with sexual chemistry and energy as their conversation meandered from light to deep and all points in between.

"Your dad and grandmother are good?"

Lightly stroking the back of his hand with her thumb, she brought him up-to-date on the two who'd raised her after her mother opted on her new man. "Granny's yet Granny and acting like eighty-five's the new fifty." Her sixty-three-year-old father was still a rolling stone, procreating wherever he roamed. "His latest and greatest? I have a five-year-old sister." Having nine siblings from six different women, Senaé gave her father props for loving and taking care of his brood despite his inability to settle himself with one woman. "Tell me how you journeyed into the transportation business."

He released her hand long enough to squeeze her thigh. "I love fast cars and fiery women."

Her side-eye left him laughing.

"I know your father used to prop you on his lap when you were little and let you "drive" in parking lots of abandoned buildings. Is your business partially in honor of him?"

She felt soft, warm and wanted when he lifted her hand and kissed it.

"Absolutely. I remember rolling with my dad when he drove professionally. I loved it as much as I did being up under the hood with him. Back then, the garage was our man cave. Moms would pitch a fit when we came in the house greasy and dirty."

She smiled, grateful he held onto good memories. "Cars are in your blood."

"Mos def," he agreed. "After football and our marriage went sideways I worked odd jobs, but I was real dissatisfied and knew I had to leave Chi-Town. When you moved to Dallas, I flipped a coin and let it lead me. Heads? California. Tails? Tennessee. Cali got me. So I'm a year in and rolling home from a club near one-thirty in the morning when I see some big dude and a woman on the side of the freeway wilding out, fussing and cussing. I was gonna keep it moving until she hauled off and pimp-slapped him."

She laughed until he added, "He punched her back. I was like 'hell, naw, you don't hit a female'. So I pulled over and wound up in the business."

Massaging the back of his neck, Senaé sat fascinated at Lex discovering the woman was a rising star new to Black Hollywood out their raising ruckus with a rap legend.

"Man, you could sniff the liquor and weed a mile away. I tried talking them both down, but dude flared up when she said his bed game was lame and tried to go in on her again."

"What happened?"

"I had to draw on him."

Senaé leaned away in open-mouthed astonishment.

"Unfortunately, some brothers'll respect a bullet before they do a woman. Anyhow, he left her stranded out there and told her to walk her 'silly ass' home. Remember now, this was before the days of ride share companies. Mama Peaches raised me better than to leave a sister waiting on a cab at dark-forty in the morning. I took her home."

She wasn't surprised at his declining the starlet's offer to pay for the ride and his silence.

"She didn't want that mess leaked to the press, but I gave her my word it wouldn't. The next day she calls asking can I get her to an audition in forty minutes. Apparently, her license was suspended and, thanks to all that wilding out, she'd overslept."

"So, you did it, and…?"

"As they say, it's history. I ended up being her driver. She paid real money. I bought a suit, a sedan. She fed other clients to me. That, plus my pro-sports connections had my client roster growing and rolling with Black Hollywood. She was good for me."

The tilt in his voice had Senaé leaning close, peering into his face as he drove. "Ooo, you got with her didn't you?" His shy smile was proof. "Who in Black Hollywood did you get busy in bed with, Lex? Come on. Tell me."

"Baby, that was two decades ago, but she's still in the business and deserves that silence. Plus, I can't have you clowning every time you see her on the screen."

"Lex, you're a Hollywood ho?"

His roaring laughter tickled her funny bone. "Naw, babe, nothing like that. She was the only one. I walk a straight line and don't fraternize."

"So…if I was on the side of the road scrapping with some dude in the middle of the night, would you play Ryde-the-Knight, deliver *moi* and take me home and satisfy me sexually?"

His humor left, and his baritone hit an even lower note. "First off, if a man ever hit you he'd better hide his ass in hell."

That secret place in her soul felt delicious at his protectiveness.

"Second, my woman's complete satisfaction means something to me. And, I don't mean just sexually. That's where most men start. But I'm fully coming for you, Senaé Dawson. I want your body and your heart."

When he raised her hand to his lips, kissing it, her heart danced with the heat and pleasure of promise.

CHAPTER EIGHT
Lex

*J*asmine and lavender.

Tolerant of her need to visit every boutique they encountered on Catalina Island, he'd pulled out his wallet on multiple occasions ready to buy whatever elicited her admiration. But she'd repeatedly declined, claiming she was simply window shopping until Senaé's holding a smoky purple bottle beneath his nose changed the game.

"I *love* this blended oil! And it's hard to find."

Inhaling, he was whisked back to his garage and the teasing foreplay of kissing his way up her thigh. "What is it?"

The salesperson's quick commandeering of the conversation spun them down an unnecessary path about proprietary benefits.

Lex had been sold at the first whiff of the scent similar enough to be the seductive fragrance marking the magic between Senaé's legs. "You take debit or credit?"

"We accept both, sir."

She'd instantly objected. "Lex, baby, for real. I just want to enjoy my date day with you. There's no need to buy me anything."

Handing his card to the salesperson, he took pleasure in advising, "Woman, that's not for you. It's for me."

"What? Why?"

The hot grin lifting the corner of his lips was his reply.

"Oh…"

He appreciated the way she returned his heated stare, the warm light that lit her eyes as he slowly slid his gaze down her body to rest in the vicinity of that velvet valley. He leisurely licked his lips before looking up again, noting the accelerated rise and fall of her breasts.

"Here you are, sir." The salesperson handing him a small, handled shopping bag interrupted his visual indulgence. "Just so you know should you accidentally ingest any, no worries. This particular jasmine and lavender blend is absolutely edible and has a delightful flavor."

Hungrily eyeing the woman he wanted as his own, he answered honestly. "Yes, ma'am. I've tasted it. I know."

As a sole proprietor who rarely took time off, their day together was a treat, and one he definitely needed. They'd toured the island via a scenic drive before feasting on ocean-fresh seafood paired with high-end wine. Dolled up in a peach and ivory dress that had her curves on swerve, she'd passed on the rock climbing he'd tried to entice her with. Now, suited and fashionably booted in jeans and a jersey rather than his typical tailored suits or slacks, he sat, legs sprawled, on the glass-bottom catamaran privately chartered from one of his Black Chamber of Commerce brothers, completely relaxed.

"Lex, did you see that?"

"Mmm-hmm," he falsified, watching excitement

lighting the face of the woman beside him. He was too occupied studying her to completely care about marine life.

They'd reconnected in a way that defied lost time. Spirits uniting on new planes that merely heightened and reinforced past familiarity, theirs was a dynamic synergy and energy. That energy elucidated an absence he'd often experienced.

For the most part, my life's on point.

Successful business. Financial solvency. Every car he wanted. And any material thing he needed. But that soft, feminine force that he desired in his home and his heart was missing. Female friends didn't fill the absence. This woman had at one time, and he wanted her again.

"Lex, stop lying and look."

It wasn't his first ride on a glass-bottom boat, and he couldn't feign exaggerated interest in the murky waters below. Still, to humor her, he leaned forward to see what she saw. "I'm looking, baby, at what?"

She sucked her teeth. "You missed it. I swear it was a rainbow fish."

He tried not to laugh, but couldn't prevent it. "That species isn't on this continent."

"I know that, Mister Man. That's why I wanted you to see if you saw it, too."

Sliding an arm about her waist, he leaned in. "Yeah, okay... *What's that!*" His sudden jerking pitched them forward, causing Senaé to scream.

"Lex!"

Pulling her away from the edge of the seat, he sat back laughing.

"You play too much," she fussed, swatting his leg.

"Did you really think you'd fall through the bottom? Or that I'd let you?"

"No, but I don't need you startling the ish out of me."

"You're scared of water—"

"I am not," she insisted.

"You're scared to fly," he continued over her objection.

"Lex, again, stop the lies. I love to fly. I'm just deathly afraid of heights."

"See. That right there. Makes less than little sense."

He loved the musicality in her laughter and—after the misfortune of being with women attracted to his bank account more than him—he valued her genuineness.

"Whatever, Mr. Ryde."

Reaching for her hand, he stroked it. "You offended?"

"Lex, you know me better than that. I can take a joke like a man."

"Thank God you're all woman." He pulled her towards him, lowering his mouth to hers. Her lips were lush, and he took his time with their kiss, allowing it to transmit need that transcended the physical. She intoxicated him in ways no other woman could, and he felt off-balance when she eased away before he was ready for that connection to end.

Her voice was thick, with the slightest shake to it. "What're we doing, Lex?"

"Letting it do what it do."

"No…not happening. I'm not sixteen anymore and have zero room for randomness. Every choice in my life needs to be worth the work and the risk. We've been down 'Let It Do' Drive before and I can't take a repeat of that same trip."

He passed a hand over his goatee, acknowledging her sentiment as valid. "My bad on the word choice. I'm not suggesting randomness. All I'm saying is we let this happen." He angled himself so that they were face-to-face. "As for trip taking, that was yesterday. Today's today. I've changed." He laid a hand over her heart. "You've changed. We're not repeating our past. We're grown folks who know want we want, what works, and what won't. So let's do different." One finger beneath her chin, he lifted it. He kissed the hollow of her throat before speaking softly in her ear. "Keep it one hundred and tell me what you need now that I couldn't give you back then."

He didn't push when she lapsed into silence. Rather, he watched emotions play and parade across her face until—with a sigh—she spoke her one-word requirement.

"Forever."

He held her gaze and simply nodded.

"One hundred for real? Getting penis isn't a problem. It's easy to get whenever I need it, but I'm good with not being somebody's side chick, or a friend with benefits. I don't have time for games and, for me, that's all that is. So, yes, a possible forever is what I'm asking, Lex. If you're down for that, fine. If not? Let's handle this heat between us, get our orgasms and be gone. But what you're not going to do is take my heart and drop it off somewhere for someone else to heal."

Tenderly, he wiped her lone tear.

"I'm serious, Lex. I can't love you again and have you leave."

He understood she didn't mean spatially or geographically, but that departure that occurred when souls separated and hearts divided. Cupping her face in one hand, he peered into her eyes, wanting to communicate the depths of his decision and desire. "I can't give you guarantees on anything except me, Senaé. I'm an imperfect person, but trust me, baby, I'm all in. 'Til the wheels fall off. If that happens? We get out and walk. You down for that?"

"I am."

"You want me enough to try again?"

"Yes, Lex."

Her affirming response clashed with her facial expression, causing him to sense she was sitting on a secret he might need to hear. "Say whatever it is you're not saying, Naé."

Her toying with the soft curls of her shoulder-length wig and exhaling a long streaming breath had him on alert for the serious.

"Do you still want children, Lex?"

He paused before answering. "I'm a man, and men like to leave legacy. But honestly, at this stage in my life it's not a priority. However, I'm open to the idea *with* the right woman. You mind answering the same question for me?"

"I've always wanted children...even after we broke up."

"Why didn't you have any?"

"Because I can't."

Her soft admission carried the weight of countless bricks. He could only sit back and take her truth in. "I must be missing something, seeing as how you were pregnant with my child."

"Yes, and losing him or her the way I did in that accident messed me up inside. And I don't just mean emotionally. Physically? There was a lot of...damaged tissue and scarring." She shrugged as if accepting fate again. "I can't conceive."

He covered her hands with his. "Damn, baby, I'm sorry. When did you find out?"

"After the miscarriage."

Her hesitation had him feeling some kind of something. "When, precisely?"

"The doctor told me at a follow-up appointment...a month or so after the accident."

He stared at her a long moment before slowly releasing her hands. Leaning forward, legs wide, he propped elbows on his thighs and massaged his forehead as if clarity were trapped there. "You knew this when we were married and said nothing?"

"We were technically married but messed up and emotionally divorced already, Lex. You were dealing with your eye and your leg...and the inability to play football anymore. You were wilding out with the weed and the drinking—"

"So, your silence was my doing?" Looking at the scene the glass bottom allowed, he felt as cloudy as the ocean beneath his Timberland-booted feet.

"No, I own that. But like you said, Lex, we were young and dumb. I made the stupid choice not to tell you because you wanted children, and Mama Peaches..."

Her voice trailed off, leaving him to side-eye her at the mention of his foster mother. "What about Mama Peaches?"

She shook her head. "Never mind. We have enough to deal with right here."

Sitting up with a sigh, he sprawled his legs out before him and leaned back, sunshades on, hands folded atop his flat abs as he watched the cloudless, California sky. "These past two decades I've been carrying our divorce on my shoulders like the fault was all mine. I don't excuse me, but your role is just as big. You left 'cause you were holding a lie. Am I right?"

"I never lied, Lex—"

"Call it selective silence," he gritted, running a hand over his head. "Let me go out on a limb and say you agreed to our divorce and left for Dallas because you were feeling guilty for withholding this from me."

He watched her tuck her feet beneath her before responding.

"I felt like less than a woman, Lex."

His voice rumbled low in his chest. "I didn't feel like less than a man? Yeah…sit with that," he remarked in her responsive silence. Time stretched and contorted itself into uncomfortable configurations as words went unsaid. He was first to break. "Point blank period: you didn't trust me to want you based on the fact that we couldn't have another baby." The muscles in his jaw twitched. "I never showed you I was a better man than that?"

On the verge of cussing, he wanted the advantage of anger; but as easily as anger came it left. His voice softened. "It never crossed your mind that I was a foster and might be willing to foster or adopt?"

He studied her profile as she averted her gaze to watch the moving ocean.

"Look at me, Senaé." He shifted her physically when she failed to, forcing the confrontation. "Let's set it straight. I made mistakes. I learned from them. Trust me when I tell you, if I'm with you, I'm with you. Rain or shine. No disrespect, but I'm not your stepdad or your pops. I'm not the dude who'll put you out your own house, and I'm not the rolling stone you can't hold. Yes, we messed up but," a finger beneath her chin, he lifted it, "I'm here. I'm not your temporary fix. If you want me, I'm not going anywhere. Got it?"

"Yes."

"Good. You say you want forever from me? Ask about my needs."

He noted the way her breasts swelled when she deeply inhaled before softly inquiring, "Lexington Ross Ryde, what do you need from me?"

He removed his shades to ensure she glimpsed the center of his soul. "Everything. Your hurts. Your pains and victories. If you want me as your man forever for real this go around, you don't get to keep your trust from me. If you give me Senaé, give me her everything."

"Back then, secrecy was my only defense, still...I ask you to please forgive me for that. But now?"

He felt the tenderness in her touch when she stroked his jaw.

"You can have all of me." She punctuated her promise with a sweet but brief kiss.

Objecting to its brevity, he reinforced his hold about her waist, reclaiming her lips and deftly increasing the heat and the depth of a kiss that was mutual penitence and promise. With the tip of his tongue he prodded her mouth, seeking entrance. She opened, gently sucking him in.

Damn, I've missed my woman.

A firm hold about her waist, he lifted her so that she straddled him.

Man, you 'bout to turn these fish sideways doing nasty things out here on the ocean?

Rationale and reason cut through the heat and the need, reminding him they lacked absolute privacy. He couldn't go all in the way he wanted. Loving and licking. Stripping them both butt-naked. Spreading her wide, deeply immersing and riding like his name depended on it would have to wait until behind closed doors. How to keep it on lock until then was more task than he cared to manage. Feeling unleashed need in the warmth of her skin, and the subtle movement of her hips had already caused him to stiffen and thicken.

He released their kiss only to trace a path down her neck with tongue and lips.

"Keep moving these hips like this and see if we don't wind up in a predicament," he rumbled, easing the hem of her dress up so that it pooled in his lap, exposing the chocolate satin of her skin.

Her words were jagged, breathless. "Keep touching me and you're going to need to satisfy me right here."

The thought of making love to her beneath an open sky was wild, luscious, causing a surge in his already rigid erection. "Bae, trust. If it weren't for this boat crew, I'd already be inside of you," he rasped, his wide palms working their way over her abundant curves—shapely legs, firm thighs—coming to rest on the round, ripeness of her behind. Her lace thong exposing her flesh, had him groaning and greedy. "Damn, woman, you feel good."

"I taste that way, too."

"Yeah, bae, you do." Memory led him to a tender place beneath her left ear. Sucking firmly, he was rewarded with her soft sighs. One hand gripping her behind, anchoring her firmly in place, he allowed the other to wander her body until cupping her breast. Slipping his hand beneath the neckline of her dress, he gently kneaded and stroked, causing her to moan.

He felt her reach for the front closure of her lacy bra.

"Naw, baby, leave that. It's to my advantage," he husked, rubbing the fabric against her nipples, eliciting her gasp at the material's added friction. Lowering his head, he treated her to tender nips of his teeth, the hot torture of his tongue, until the movement of her hips increased as if under their own volition.

Still gripping her behind, he pushed his pelvis upward, pressing his hardness against her lace-covered velvet. When she widened her legs, wrapping them around his back, he wanted to plunge into her and let the ride begin. Instead, he reminded himself he was a grown ass man whose self-control was to both their benefits.

"Oh...my...*God*, Lex..." she breathed as he slowly ground against her feminine center so that her breath caught, then released in a rush.

"What, baby?" Simultaneously, he stroked the lacy thong covering her femininity while increasing the serpentine movements of his pelvis to escalate her pleasure.

"You're...wicked..."

He groaned before whispering, "And you're wet."

The sudden sound of footsteps on the stairs

brought their sexcapades to an unwanted end.

Hurriedly, she righted her dress and repositioned herself, sitting demurely on his lap.

"Pardon me, Mr. Ryde, but we'll be dockside in five minutes tops."

"Thank you."

"You're welcome, sir."

He waited for the shipmate to disappear before returning his attention to his woman. "I'm not trying to cheapen us, or you, but—"

He grit his teeth when she managed to slide a hand beneath the closure of his jeans.

Stroking the boxer briefs enclosing him, she finished his thought. "We need a room. You have condoms?"

Exhaling loudly, he kissed her deeply before confirming. "For you, baby, I do."

CHAPTER NINE

Senaé

Hotel Metropole's luxuries were noted only cursorily. Seated in the lobby—body and emotions rioting and roiling—her focus was devoted to the man completing their registration process. Kind, huge-hearted, his soft-spoken, easy nature were surface layers of a complex and powerful spirit. Watching his quiet, self-assured interaction with hotel staff—his manner of handling himself, and that confident but laidback sex appeal—had her falling. Hard. Again.

Her heart raced as he accepted key cards from the front desk attendant before turning in her direction. Hooking up in a hotel with a man wasn't her regular mode of conduct.

There's nothing "regular" about him.

As if life were on replay, she wanted round two with Lex. Want brought her here, greedy to handle whatever treasures the bedroom brought them.

Sex. In a hotel. With her ex-husband?

"This is some straight up movie plot, in-a-novel kind of nonsense."

It felt lurid. Dangerously delicious.

"Downright ho'ish," she commented, amazed at how swiftly his laidback sexiness transformed into blazing and blatant. Subconsciously, she licked her lips, seeing his smooth, panther-like stalk of a walk that communicated he meant business.

"Ready, baby?"

His voice was thick with sexual need. Accepting his hand, she stood, allowing him to pull her close. His closeness and the clandestine thrill at a hotel situation with her ex had her arousal on full blast. "Ready and still wet," she whispered, subtly moving her body against his.

"Well, *damn*, Miss Dawson. Can we get this?"

Staring into the heated appetite in his gold-toned eyes, she inwardly melted. "What're we getting, Lex, other than sex?"

A hand at her waist, he nuzzled her throat before quietly speaking in her ear. "Love, baby. All day and night if need be. We're *making love*. Trust me."

Locating their room was easy. Containing an inferno until there proved challenging. Their door barely closed before he had her pressed against it—his lips on her throat, a hand on her breast, a hand palming her hips. She squirmed and burned for him in a way that felt ridiculous. A runaway train, she cursed her bladder's sudden insistence.

"Bathroom...I need...to use..." she managed on a broken breath. "Lex," she practically moaned when he—as if he hadn't heard a word—continued torturing her flesh.

He groaned against her neck. "Are you serious?"

"Yes."

"Your kidneys are killing me."

Taking his hand, she placed it in the valley between her thighs. "You die, you won't get this sexual healing." She kissed him in a way that conveyed absolute confidence in the rightness of them. "I'll be right back."

She shivered as his hand she'd captured between her legs massaged her with firm but gentle movements as he breathed in her ear,

"Stay too long and I'm coming for you."

Pulling herself from his hold, she stepped into the bathroom, closed the door, and handled her business before leaning against the sink trying to calm her racing heartbeat.

"You are way too horny and hyped," she told her mirrored reflection, crediting her six-month abstinence when in truth it was all Lex. He'd kept a part of her heart that no other man could have or hold. The handful of relationships she'd had felt like imposters in the interim. There was a flatness to them simply because not one of those lovers had been him. She'd come full circle back to her ex-husband.

"And I refuse to be tangy and tart in the reunion." Grabbing a washcloth and complimentary toiletries, she made quick business of refreshing herself and brushing her teeth in the absence of her full armory of barely there lingerie, "potions and lotions" and sexy toy-things.

Honey, he's about to get the full, natural me.

Spitting toothpaste foam in the sink, she examined herself, quickly.

Forty was far from twenty, and her skinny had left along with her scrawny. Turning left then right, she scoped a body that had collected twenty-plus pounds since Lex last loved it. Breasts, thighs, behind and hips seemed to be grand prize winners of that expansiveness.

"Honey, you're a Black woman. It is what it is. Five-feet-one or not, that booty gonna be big."

Such was life and her failure to frequent the gym. Time hadn't been an adversary, but gravity wasn't a friend. She wasn't picture-perfect, but that Black Don't Crack mystique had obviously graced her face, and she had genetics to thank that—even if she wasn't lifted high—her stuff wasn't hanging.

"Girl, you're good, and forty is too old for foolery."

This man wants me, not a Barbie.

She was ready for him with all of her heat, her need, sexual appetite and abilities. And love. Hot, healed love that took the past and made it stepping stones to the present.

And that penis.

"You've been around Dove too much." Snickering at her foolishness, she opened the bathroom door, hungry to love her man. The smile she wore got stuck thanks to a virile vision.

On the opposite side of the room stood Lex, natural and naked, sporting nothing except the Black is Beautiful skin he'd been born in.

"Kayla, I appreciate you going by the house and getting Jazz for your favorite Uncle Lex." His being on a call gave her the privilege of visually ingesting him.

My...oh...my...

His naked beauty left her speechless.

Time and God had been good to him; and he'd clearly put in the work to maintain that NFL physique he'd been blessed with. Certainly, changes had occurred. But from her perspective, maturation merely enhanced the fact that he was all man.

Her mind went Florida Evans on her and she mentally yelled,

"Damn...damn...DAMN!"

"I'll swing by and get her on my way in tomorrow. You know where her food is? Cool. Peace." Ending the call, he turned towards her, granting her a full-frontal vision of chocolate manliness. "You alright, baby?"

Watching him extract condoms from his wallet, she couldn't reply. She was too busy lusting. All of her thirsts were on alert as he swaggered towards her with unswerving confidence and grown man power. Fully erect and ready, his masculine beauty had her mouth watering.

Lawd, that's some good and plenty.

Might have been her hormones and her hunger, but it appeared as if—like her healthier hips—that treasure between his legs had expanded over the years.

God, I'mma need much Vaseline and that two-letter jelly.

Pulling her gaze from his man glory, her breath felt trapped in her chest as their eyes met, as he approached, his sexual need sweltering and intense. His expression had her shook, as if she'd never been wanted this way by any man.

Standing toe-to-toe, her body to his, they stared at each other, breath catching, both trapped in a kind of foreplay she'd never experienced. Her whole self shivered when he tenderly stroked a finger down her cheek before pressing that small foil packet into her hand. She accepted it, understanding the gift of control he'd given.

Her gaze never leaving his face, she opened the packet before reaching down to boldly possess him. She seductively smiled as the muscles in his body tightened and a slow hiss escaped his lips at her slowly massaging downward and up again. With languid kisses to his chest, his nipples and abdomen, she made sheathing him part of their foreplay and his pleasure.

She loved the hunger and heat in his touch when he gripped her hips and moved her backward into the bathroom while kissing her senseless. Hands wandering beneath her dress, he lifted it overhead and dropped it as if a nuisance.

"Damn."

His visual devouring turned her insides into hot liquid. His touch left her shivering.

Her head lolled back and she inhaled on a gasp as Lex licked and nipped a path of pleasure down her body. Squatting to remove her lacy underwear, he treated her to penetrating, explorative kisses.

This man has a million-dollar mouth.

Deftly skilled, he worked those full lips and talented tongue to her advantage. Her belly, her thighs quivered in response to his spreading her, lapping her intimate jewel in a way that was worshipful and possessive. His merciless, masterful tongue had her moaning and groaning, her fingernails digging into his skin. A prisoner to his pleasuring, she felt herself being literally lifted, Lex standing and hoisting her body so that she maintained her in-his-face position.

Draping her legs over his shoulders, her moans affirmed her ecstasy as Lex—relentless in his feasting—carefully walked them to the shower.

The room ricocheted with her pleasure and the sounds of running water he turned on. He had her so senseless she didn't bother to remove her wig as Lex walked them beneath the showerhead and warm water burst against her back.

The dual sensations of warm water and his hot tongue mesmerizing the love between her legs left her panting, gyrating as he licked her into oblivion. Within moments her pleasure poured onto his tongue. The room echoed with her screams of ultimate satisfaction.

Unable to catch her breath, her body collapsed in his strong arms. Beyond sublime, she felt utterly useless as Lex lowered her, anchoring her legs about his back. Arms around his neck, she clutched him as if her sole stability.

"*Lex…*"

"What, baby?"

Intended words were lost when he leaned her against the shower wall to gently tug at a lace-covered nipple with his teeth. The sensation hit the pit of her stomach and caught her fading orgasm.

"*Oh…God…*"

Fingers trembling, she fumbled with her bra closure until managing to free herself to him. Her whole body quivered when his mouth clamped about her, sucked her in.

Gripping the back of his head, she was suddenly conscious of the weight of her drenched wig. She snatched it from her head and threw it, where she didn't care, when feeling the thickness of him positioned at her entrance. She widened her thighs in welcome.

"Welcome back where you belong."

Her voice was sultry, ragged; her invitation was temporarily rejected. She breathed in luscious agony as he chose a different penetration. One finger, then another, he slid inside of her, tenderly manipulating places still pulsating with prior pleasure.

"*Ohhh…damn…*Lex…baby, I can't take it…"

"You can." As if her pleasure was his, he took his time stroking, coaxing her femininity in sync with his lathing and loving her breasts.

She'd never experienced multiple releases with a man. Rising, shaking and quaking, she felt delirious when her body detonated again. Her shrill cries were pure testimony. Its piercing notes hadn't faded when she felt him giving what she craved and missed most: him.

Her eyes clamped shut with the absurd sensations flooding her flesh at his slow, deliberate entrance. Breath caught in both of their throats at the pure deliciousness. Overwhelmed, Senaé tightened her hold about his neck and buried her face beneath his ear. Her back to the shower wall she felt helpless, unable to function except to hold on as—gripping her hips— he pushed deeply into her with a control that defied his need and greed.

His push became her pulse. Her hips matched his movements. Their momentum and pace accelerated as both, hot and high, rode ocean waves into pure paradise. When he slammed a palm against the granite wall as his body seized before offering a searing torrent of pure ecstasy, she reeled with the shockwaves of orgasmic bliss that ripped through her body. Again.

The vibrant sound of their shared fulfillment was a synchronized symphony. Like a sweet lullaby it rocked her to the core, but not as much as his jagged whispering.

"I love you, Senaé."

Too weak to speak or think, she held onto the love of her life as a tear slid from the corner of her eye.

Exhausted in his arms, she lay in bed, nails languidly raking the hair on his chest. Beyond complete, she was…

"Whipped."

"What's that?"

"Nothing."

"Naw, woman, I heard you admit your body got dealt with."

"It absolutely did." A lazy laugh spilled from her lips as she looked at him. She liked who and what she saw: her first ever lover supremely content in the afterglow of them. The intimacies enjoyed in their youthful marriage couldn't compare to being intimately, ultimately loved by his adult, sexy self.

"You're shook, huh?"

"Yes, Lex, and you're a braggart."

His laugh was content, confident. "I'm just saying, baby. Your man has talents."

Pushing up and away from his chest, she stared down at him. "I don't even want to know with whom or how you honed them."

"Doesn't matter 'cause here and forward you're the only woman getting it."

"That's a promise?" she purred.

"Yes, ma'am. I'm not tryna see you go to jail."

"What're you talking about?"

"Oh, trust! I remember you getting suspended for going in on Jalisa Morgan and snatching a plug from her hair."

Senaé had to laugh. "First of all, it was weave or horsetail. Second, I was a stupid teen in the tenth grade and chick was pushing up on my man."

"It was a simple hug on my birthday, babe."

"She needed her tongue in your mouth to complete that hug, huh?"

"She kissed my cheek, Naé."

"That's not how I remember it," she commented, flopping down beside him.

She crossed her arms over her naked breasts when he copped the position she'd just relinquished, pushing up on an elbow and spiraling a finger in her damp, shoulder-length braids that had begun to unravel courtesy of their shower. "That's 'cause you were jealous."

"Note to Lexington: I still don't share."

"That makes two of us. You. Me. No friends with benefits. You down with that?"

"I am." She feigned a menacing look when warning, "No, side chicks."

"No, side dick."

"Really, Lex?"

"'Ey, I'm keeping it one-hundred. The monogamy you want from me, I want from you. I'm not having another man in, on, or near anything that belongs to Ryde and Company."

"Oh, so now I'm a possession?"

"Bae, you're a prize."

She clutched the blanket when he moved her arm aside to flatten his tongue against her left breast and take his sweet time licking his way up its mound, over the caramel-colored birthmark decorating her flesh.

Tracing its outline with his tongue, his chuckle was smoky, thick. "Yeah, sweetheart, you grew."

Reaching between their bodies, she gripped his thickness: her new addiction. "So did you."

Laughing, he clutched her hips and rolled onto his back, bringing her with him.

She lay against his chest, content in the magic of them. "Lex?"

"Hmm?"

She kissed his chest and teased him with her tongue before quietly questioning, "Did I tell you I love you when you told me?"

"You were too busy screaming." His mocking her wails of ecstasy left her laughing.

"I love you, Lexington Ryde-the-Knight who rides me like a king." She sealed her sentiment with a kiss.

"Thank you, Queen. How long've we been apart?"

Squinting at him, she wondered if his inquiry was rhetorical or due to his volcanic orgasming causing a temporary lack of brain oxygen. "Really, babe? Try twenty years."

"That's how many orgasms I owe you before your trip ends."

She thrilled at his devilish grin. "You realize I leave tomorrow, right?"

"You already ripped three." Gyrating beneath her—one hand in her hair easing her head back as his tongue treated her nipples to gentle flicks—he was ready to set her on the road towards his goal. "Let's get busy on the seventeen."

"Can we rest first?"

"You never wanted rest when we were married," he teased.

"Well, we're not anymore, and I'm not eighteen."

"You want to be?"

"Eighteen?"

"Married."

She stared down at him a silent, prolonged moment. "Stop playing, Lex."

His voice was intentionally quiet when suggesting, "Think about it."

Tongue-tied, she had no coherent response other than peering into his eyes before kissing him, hoping to touch and taste the flavor of his suggestion. It was sweet. Filled with honey and heat. The more she tasted, the more she wanted as his hands stroked down her back, rested on her behind. She groaned at his massaging grip, his pressing her downward against his "man gift."

She felt herself ripening.

Girl, don't you ever go six months without sex again.

He had her triggering.

Unapologetic, she reached for the foil-wrapped square on the bedside stand. Ripping it open, she took her time sheathing him.

"*Damn*, baby…you make putting on protection sweet."

Smiling, she kissed him, mystified by their reunion and her ever-present responsiveness to his sexiness and magnetism. She wanted to rest, and her body certainly could use it. But he was her stimuli and loving him had unleashed something wild. After her prior triplicate of orgasms, she had no expectations of climaxing. She was absolutely fine with making this solely about him.

Opening herself, she took Lex in and sighed with his satisfying depth and strength, love and length. Riding slowly and rhythmically, she knew she'd come home where *she* belonged. Any lover she'd had outside of him had been purely counterfeit, strong and wrong.

Our fit is tailor-made. Perfect.

The purity of that truth settled sweetly over her soul. His touch, his kisses, his holding her hips—synchronizing himself with her sinuous movements—had her moaning, glowing, and flowing towards a fourth trip to paradise. And a second chance at this life.

CHAPTER TEN
Lex

Can I get one more day?
He'd asked. She'd answered by opting to fly home versus taking the train, giving them the gift of added time. They'd spent that gift on lovemaking, and breakfast on the beach before leaving Hotel Metropole and heading back to Santa Monica. What was meant to be a quick stop at A Royal Ryde to pick up Jazz, turned into Senaé's meeting Kayla, Khaleed, and other staff. She'd insisted on a full tour of his enterprise, expressing awe and appreciation for his accomplishments that embarrassed the shy part of him even while bolstering his pride.

"I like the size of this desk." In his office, she'd walked the perimeter of his oversized furniture as if measuring it. Sitting sexily on top, she'd pulled him between her legs, kissing him in a way that left him wanting to dismiss staff for the day.

"Keep it up and we'll be back here after-hours handling business."

Laughing, she'd released him, leaving him to readjust himself in his pants.

Leaving A Royal Ryde, they'd opted on a walk on the Santa Monica pier that afternoon. An early dinner had been capped off with soul delving and desperately good lovemaking edging them closer to his giving-you-twenty-orgasms goal.

Grinning, he got lost in memory of her sexual desires and abilities. Her carnal appetite and confidence hadn't waned with age; if anything, it had increased. It was his duty and delight satisfying her needs repeatedly. Now, days later, his love and lust in the palm of her manicured hands, mere thought of their lovemaking caused him to swell.

Man, you better focus before you drop these weights on your head.

Bench-pressing in a spare bedroom remodeled into a home gym that proved perfect for late night or early morning sessions like this, Lex regulated his breathing, counted reps. His count went off track as thoughts of his woman, once again, sauntered in.

Bruh, you're whipped.

He had no issues admitting that or the fact that he was sprung and missed her as if years had passed instead of days since they'd last made love in sinfully erotic ways. He still imagined her taste on his tongue, the deep pleasure of her sugar walls clutching him. He'd suspended familiarity and relearned her body, taking his time to worship it and discover new sensitivities. The physical was lit, but he missed her smile, her laugh, the gentleness of her touch equally as much and questioned whether or not he was suited for a commuter relationship. Already, he was backed up, bothered and blue, and overdue. He desperately needed Miss Grown and Gottdamn Sexy's touch.

"Incoming call from Adrian Collins."

Jazz barked at the automated voice coming through the surround sound system and interrupting the music meant to motivate this early morning workout that had Lex wet with sweat.

Replacing the weights on their mount, he caught

his breath and surrendered to the canine kisses of his Husky licking sweat from his face.

"Okay, girl, I heard it," Lex assured as the automated voice repeated itself. With his phone already synced to the sound system, he pressed a button on the nremote to accept the call, electing to remain hands-free as he launched into a round of crunches. "What it do, short stack?"

At six-foot-six, his foster brother Adrian Collins out-measured him by four inches. Still, being ten years older, Lex didn't miss a chance to get his big brother digs in.

Adrian's laughter was good-natured and indulgent. "It do what it do, old man. Why you breathing all hard first thing in the morning when you're woman-less? You doing things by your solo self?"

"Oh, you a funny so-and-so with the clown jokes. What do you want, A.C.? If *you* had a woman you wouldn't be calling."

"See how you do, Lex Ryde? Why you coming for me?"

Their brotherly laughter blended in tones, masculine and deep.

"And why you up so early, Ryde-the-Knight? It's eight-something here in Philly, so that's five'ish California time."

"Gotta get this fitness in before this busy day runs away from me. On the real, A.C., whaddup with it?" Lex questioned, the big brother in him trying not to read more into this morning call than merited.

Of all the housemates and fosters he'd known while in Mama Peaches' care, Adrian was the one he held onto the hardest. A mere toddler when his mother left, Adrian had latched onto Lex who'd demonstrated an uncanny ability to calm the child when fretting and distressed. Within days of his mother's abandonment, Adrian was prattling nonstop toddler gibberish and following Lex wherever he went. Lonely for the siblings he'd lost, Lex embraced Adrian as if his own gift. Godsends to each other, they'd maintain their brotherly bond over the years, but early morning calls rarely factored in.

"You straight?" Lex rasped, going in on his abdominal work with a vengeance.

My baby likes licking these abs. Gotta keep 'em tight and right.

"Yeah, I'm good."

"Try again. And this time…remember who… you're talking to," he managed between reps.

"Man, Lex, that auction busted a brother."

He listened to his God-sent sibling explaining how Priscilla—a woman he had history with—won his bid. It was old, already known news to Lex. What was fresh was the fact that Adrian had been instantly attracted to the woman who'd engaged in and lost a bidding war to Adrian's ex.

"Here's the crazy part, Lex. Daphne lives here in Philly—"

"Who's Daphne?"

"Man, that exercising is affecting your brain ability. Daphne Turner is the woman who lost the bid."

"'Ey, you never…said her…name."

"Well, I just did. Anyhow! When I left Chicago after the auction, we ended up on the same flight home. *Together*. Wild, or what?"

"Or destiny. She has…you spinning?"

"For real. My mind's all messed up. And pause on the push-ups or whatever the hell you doing. Breathing all hard like we're phone sexing or something."

Laughing, Lex took a break, sprawling flat on his back and wiping his face. "A.C., your mind's a mess on the daily, so how's this Daphne situation different?"

"There *you* go with the clown jokes," Adrian cracked before quietly confessing an uncommon attraction that had him hemmed up, fighting every feeling he felt.

Again, Lex silently allowed the younger man to "unpack his chest" and put his angst on the table to be dealt with. Hearing how they'd exchanged phone numbers and departed with Adrian's promise to call, Lex was certain he never had in the three weeks since.

Hoisting himself up, Lex grabbed a sports drink from the mini refrigerator installed for his benefit. Sitting on the floor, back to his weight bench, he opened the bottle and sipped, speaking in the affirmative. "You're attracted to her, but haven't called. Because?"

"She's the kind of woman I could end up wanting more than sex with."

"Populate the blank. You're afraid of...?"

"The fact that you've watched Iyanla Vanzant."

"Aiight, Dumb-and-Dim, you called me. So, answer the question or get off my line 'cause I got better things to do than game play with you."

He felt the shift in lack of levity when Adrian answered honestly. "Man...my past didn't prepare me for love."

Their shared silence was embedded with understanding. Their mothers' abandonment had wreaked havoc on their souls and psyches. While Mama Peaches and Papa Brighton had mitigated wounds by gifting an amazing love, that didn't prevent occasional bouts of doubt and unworthiness when young. Not that he was immune, but his early marriage had aided Lex in his ability to negotiate and silence the fear of giving himself to someone in love. Despite multiple relationships, that gifting was something his foster brother had yet to experience. "A.C., you know I know. Right?"

"Yeah…you do, Ryde."

"So, trust your big bruh when I tell you some things are worth the risk, including a life with love," he remarked, beyond grateful at God's gracing he and Senaé a second chance.

"Even if it's a bust?"

"Fo' sho! Even if things don't go how you think they should or could. Be alright with it even if it turns out to be no more than a solid friendship. But the way you're talking, Miss Daphne may be the something special you're missing. Don't let what your moms did hold you hostage."

When Adrian remained silent, Lex put a little Mama Peaches in the mix. "You told her you'd call? Honor your word, A.C. Bite that bullet and be a gent."

"I'm that twenty-four-seven…but, I hear you." Adrian's sigh was resigned, yet light. "I have to call, Lex, 'cause I'm feeling this woman."

"Don't tell me. Tell Daphne."

"Yeah, alright already. So…let me get ankle-deep in your bidnezz. What happened with you and my big sis? Did Mama Peaches and Miss Geraldine let you and Senaé out that bad bid situation?"

A beep indicating another incoming call diverted Lex's attention. "A.C., hold on and let me get this." Switching over, a huge grin spread his full lips. "'Ey, baby."

"Good morning, my sexy Lexi. How're you?"

"Better now that I'm hearing your voice, but I'm missing my boo."

"Me, too. Are you ready?"

"For?"

"You better be playing with me, Lex."

His deep chuckle confirmed the fact. "Girl, you got me up all early getting my sweat in so I can be ready to watch my baby do her magic. You set?"

"Yes, but I'm nervous."

"This is what you do, Senaé, all day every day."

"I know, Lex, but a makeover on live T.V. is a whole other kind of something."

"Maybe, but that doesn't change your skillset or ability. Relax, boo, and do you. You got this, baby. Okay?"

Her words were a silken purr. "Whoever says good Black brothers don't exist is a straight up lie 'cause I got mine."

"Sho' 'nuff, you do. You all packed?"

"Yes! And I'm kid-kind-of-excited over this beauty ambassador tour. I can't wait to board that plane tomorrow." Her voice softened. "But being out east'll put me farther away from my baby."

"Distance isn't anything an airplane can't conquer. We'll work it out. Okay?"

"Okay."

"Listen, can I holla back at you in a few? I got Adrian crying on the other line."

"What's wrong with my little brother?"

Lex laughed, remembering how she used to spoil him back when. "Big Head's gonna be alright."

"Well…I hope whatever it is works out. Tell him I

said 'hi.' And don't worry about calling since I'll be on set. We can connect later."

"Sounds good. Go be great. Love you, baby."

"Love you back."

"'Ey, Naé! Wait." He let his tone dip down deep and sexy. "What color panties you got on them assets?"

"*Boy, you're ridiculous.* Bye!"

Her laughter ringing in his ears as she disconnected, he grinned, his mission to distract her from stressing accomplished. "I'm back with you, A.C."

"Must've been some woman 'cause you sounding all nighttime jazz station D.J.'ish. Who were you talking to?"

"Shuddup and focus on you. Call Daphne. Do what you need to."

"I already said I would."

"Today, knucklehead. You get zero opportunity to talk yourself out of it."

"I got it already, Lex, and you never answered my question. Did you and Senaé ditch that bid?"

Grinning, Lex took his time responding. "Who you think that was calling?"

"*What?* Man, stop lying! You and Naé are on good terms again? Come on, Lex," Adrian urged when he remained silent. "Wait…wait…wait one good damn minute! Y'all been in the bed?"

"Dude, you stupid."

"I'm not. When you got back on the line you had that pop-them-panties voice pumping."

"'Ey, watch your mouth."

"That right there confirms it! You all protective and ish. Y'all back together, *for real,* for real? Or you just handling booty bidnezz?"

"I ain't doing this with your ig'nance. Call Daphne, A.C." Disconnecting, he whistled for Jazz and left the weight room. Ignoring Adrian's calling again, Lex thoroughly enjoyed depriving his know-it-all, knuckleheaded brother of knowledge.

Stalling in the kitchen long enough to blend the strawberry-banana, quinoa, kale and pea powder smoothie Senaé made him promise he'd drink, he had to plug his nose to aid his swallowing.

He wished he'd never made the comment.

Bae, you gonna need to hit that gym if you plan on keeping up with me.

The words were said in absolute jest after some seriously rigorous lovemaking that had Senaé struggling for breath the night before she left. She'd done that opposite sex thing and incorrectly translated his statement into "you need to lose weight" despite his adamant assurance to the contrary. He didn't care that she'd put on a pound for each year of their absence. Those pounds padded the places he preferred. Her young and lush physique he once loved had sashayed itself into a full woman body he couldn't get enough of. He told and certainly showed her that her lush was his lust. Still, she'd decided she was "shaping up" despite his threats to disown her if she lost too much.

Struggling with one more sip, he placed the far from empty glass in the sink with a grimace.

"That's some straight nasty ish."

Heading for the shower, he decided he loved his woman to life, but his taste buds had limits.

Stripping, he stepped beneath the shower head, welcoming the warm downpour while saying a quick, heartfelt morning prayer. As if his "amen" signaled thoughts to commence, he was immediately bombarded with a mental "to do" list.

The monthly Black Chamber of Commerce breakfast was a few hours away.

"At least I can eat."

That crew didn't play fruit and vegetable gag reflex
drinks.

He snickered as his mind shifted to this afternoon's staff meeting that his "adopted adults", Kayla
and Khaleed, jokingly dubbed "The Lineup."

Absolutely, he lined up his drivers—male and female—ensuring the company uniform of black suits,
caps, and leather gloves were on point and spotless.
He was old school, requiring the impeccable presentation of his fleet, as well as each driver. Hair. Nails.
Every aspect was scrutinized. But he led by example.
No longer driving on the daily, rather for select clients
or when specifically requested, he still showed up
suited and booted even when business was simply
handled behind his desk. His insistence upon professionalism in decorum and presentation had granted
them a competitive edge. Lex was unapologetic about
it. Treating others with dignity, he took pride in being
a fair-minded employer and was quick to praise and
reward his staff. That didn't mean okey doke was
tolerated. A Royal Ryde hadn't achieved success by his
being lax or slack.

Truthfully, he relished the weekly opportunity to
walk "The Yard" inspecting and inventorying every vehicle like a king surveying his realm—his "like a son"
Khaleed at his side entering data on an iPad, detailing
any unreported damage that couldn't escape Lex's attention. While each vehicle was outfitted with a maintenance kit and drivers were responsible for the daily
cleaning of their whips, Khaleed's detail service arm of

the business kept them impeccable. With the benefit of Lex acting as venture capitalist, Khaleed contracted out to others but home-based at A Royal Ryde. After terminating a driver who'd systematically used a vehicle to hustle rides on the side, Lex had developed a knack for finding the minutest discrepancies in damage and mileage. With Khaleed checking speedometers and calling out figures, Lex could spit back the differences from prior entries before his right-hand man could calculate them. For Lex, "numbering" was easy. It was "that conjugating and reading" that were challenging.

His computational genius stumped Khaleed every time.

"Boss Man, when you taking that master math mind back to class?"

His adopted adults relentlessly insisted he get back in the trenches and earn his undergraduate degree. "Maybe one day," was his constant response to their badgering.

Soaping himself, Lex pushed the idea of pursuing his education aside for the pleasantries of this afternoon's inspection and inventory. More than a best business practice, the ritual afforded Lex the opportunity to calmly reflect on God's goodness.

Heavenly Father, this is all You. You took me from nothing to something. Thank You!

Stepping from the shower, his cell rang as he reached for a towel. Seeing Kayla's face on the screen, realization hit.

Damn! How'd I sleep on this?

The young woman he'd rescued from foster care bore an uncanny resemblance to his future. Slightly taller and a shade or two lighter than Senaé, Kayla was similarly shaped, possessed the same saucy, but bright smile, effervescent personality and no nonsense ways.

"Hey, baby girl. Why you up so early?"

"Morning, Uncle Lex. Your man woke me up."

"What man?" he questioned, toweling off.

"Somebody named Stanford Browning: the same rude dude who left a gazillion messages yesterday."

Lex grinned at Kayla being quick to levy a "rude" label on persons failing to mirror her sparkling ways. "I told you not to forward calls to your cell after hours. That's why we pay an answering service."

"I know, but I prefer to stay large and in charge."

Lex chuckled. "Yeah, alright. Back to Mr. Browning. Where's he calling from, and what does he want?" he asked despite something about the name sounding vaguely familiar.

"No idea. He's Secret Squirrel with his and wouldn't answer any of my questions. Let's just assume it's important since he sounds all insistent."

"Fine. I'll get with him."

"Cool. Are you on target for the Black Chamber breakfast?"

"Yes, ma'am. I'm getting dressed."

"Good. We have staff meeting today. You have inventory, *and* two conference calls after that. Khaleed will be at that automobile trade show all day tomorrow, and I'm taking Monday off."

"Since when?"

"Since I asked and you approved it. You remember, right?"

With effort he vaguely recalled a phone conversation and his approving her request in a half-conscious state following an exceedingly intense release on his last night with Senaé courtesy of the things she did with his body that had to be illegal somewhere in the U.S. "Okay…I guess."

"You know what? You're starting to scare me with the weirdness. You've been walking around grinning and whistling and all distracted. You alright?"

"Baby girl, I'm better than."

"Miss Senaé have anything to do with that?"

"Mind your twenty-six-year-old business."

They both laughed.

"On the real, I like her, Uncle Lex. You're a good man. From what I see, she's a good woman. You should make that situation solid."

Baby girl, trust, I am.

He chose to keep that thought to himself until he and Senaé had the opportunity to further discuss their future. But as for Lex, he already knew what he wanted.

"Uncle Lex, you listening?"

"What?"

"Disregard. Your mind's most likely on Miss Senaé and not this conversation, so I'm rolling over for a few more snores before heading to the office. Call Stanford Browning, please. I'll text his number. And be on time to the breakfast."

"I'm on it, baby girl. Bye."

A warrior to the end, he'd fought hard and Dyslexia hadn't gotten the best of him. His reading speed was often slower than desired, but his confidence and comprehension had reached a point where words no longer looked like a riot and a mess in print. Easily reading Kayla's text with skills acquired over the years, he laughed at her unnecessary "talking points." He knew how to address Stanford Browning. He wasn't the president, just a possible client.

Simple and straightforward with its artificially proper and clipped cadence, Stanford Browning's recorded greeting offered no clues as to what he needed, or his identity. Leaving a message, Lex decided the man would get back to him if the situation called for it.

Pulling on boxer briefs, he aimed the remote at his bedroom's flat screen and accessed a Chicago television station via the internet before preparing to shave. He put his prep on pause when hearing,

"We have internet sensation and beauty ambassador, Senaé Dawson, treating us to *Morning Makeovers in Ten Minutes or Less.* Stay tuned. That's next."

The camera panning to Senaé and her model had him feeling all kinds of things. Pride in her accomplishments. Pleasure in her successes. Gratefulness for their reunion. Awe at connecting on higher levels than even in marriage. Deep affection. Pure love. Hot lust and longing.

He hadn't missed a woman the way he missed Senaé since the days directly after their divorce when he was stuck on stupid and unable to hold a simple conversation the times she reached out. Now, he was man enough to admit he wanted *and* needed her.

For life this time.

Shaving, he allowed himself to consider their current situation and future possibilities.

We need to work out this long-distance love thing.

He was disinterested in reducing their relationship to booty call status. It had far more importance and significance. Yet, he couldn't deny the fact that his woman had reawakened the beast, had him feening for that brown sugar loving. A reverie of Senaé's sounds of sexual satisfaction, her "ooo baby, yesss, that," accompanied by that beautiful body moving rhythmically, sucking him in like a vortex from which he never wanted to be released had him going.

"Naw, dude, I can't have this," he informed what Senaé called his "man gift," willing himself not to rise to memory's lusciousness. Wiping lather from his face, he splashed cold water over his skin before patting it dry and moisturizing.

Hurrying to the walk-in closet, he eyed the clothing, pressed and draped over his suit valet. Grabbing the tailored slacks, he had one leg in when the show's announcer reintroduced Senaé's segment.

Hobble-hopping, one leg in, one out of his slacks, Lex exited the closet. He couldn't curb his grin, seeing her live and in living color. The smooth tones of her voice reached across air waves as if meant to touch only him. Not one to be left out, even Jazz got in on it, barking and whining.

Lex chuckled at his Husky's sitting, head cocked and confused, staring at the flat screen as if expecting Senaé to emerge from it.

"You look good, woman," he mumbled, fascinated and watching. He was clueless to cosmetics. That didn't keep him from being mesmerized by his woman. "My baby is a beast."

Even across the distance, her warmth and wit were on hit; and her expertise and experience were highly apparent. Her earlier bout of nerves had clearly dissipated as she easily provided tips to viewers while transforming her model's face as if a painting. And those flare-legged pants and waist-cinched blouse hugging her curves had him nearly salivating.

"Alright, boo. I see you," Lex crowed, peacock proud at her looking flawless and handling her business like a boss. Buttoning his dress shirt, he felt himself frowning as some suit-wearing dude suddenly strutted onto the set like he owned rights and privileges.

The host stumbling in her words and the expression on Senaé's face transmitted that dude's entrance was a surprise, and not exactly pleasant.

"Ol' boy's out of pocket." That surgically enhanced smile was real as a six-dollar bill. Something in his voice was familiar, but Lex was too busy heating up over the possessive hand the man placed at his woman's waist to decipher one word said.

"Apparently, viewers, my co-host wants a makeup tip or two."

His self-effacing laughter was fake as his grill. "I doubt Ms. Dawson could improve my looks. But she could do one thing for me."

Consummate professional, Senaé's face remained neutral, but reading her body language it was clear to Lex that the man had annoyed the hell out of her.

He caught the tightness in her tone. "And what's that, Stanford?"

Stanford? Browning!

Now he knew why the name seemed vaguely familiar. He'd glimpsed a Stan B. on her phone the night she'd arrived, as they sat eating chicken and waffles in the dark of morning. He'd been blowing up her phone and, with irritation, she'd silenced it. Now, there he was, needing to be busted in his head for touching a woman who wasn't his.

A vein in Lex's neck pulsed and his jaw muscles twitched as his focus darted between Senaé and the man interrupting her segment. Ice shot through his veins as Stan B. dramatically lowered to one knee, removed a ring box from his suit jacket and grabbed *his* woman's hand. His artificial New England accent was proud and loud as he asked, "Senaé, will you marry me?"

"WHAT THE HELL!"

With Jazz wildly barking at the T.V., Lex dropped onto the edge of the bed seeing nothing but red.

CHAPTER ELEVEN
Senaé

H er response had been honest. Shock. And stunned laughter.

A man she hadn't dated in over six months, who admitted to feeling nothing deep for her, suddenly wanted to propose at his place of employment? In front of television cameras? The ish was countless shades of hyper ignorant.

She'd actually glanced around the set as if Ashton Kutcher might pop up out of nowhere. It was too extra. Dove, Lovie, and Ima must have arranged for her to be punked.

"Good one, Stanford. April Fools was weeks ago. You can stop with the jokes."

If looks could kill, Senaé would've been overseeing her own funeral.

That artificially bright smile Stanford liked to shine went from embarrassed to outraged to a look that hinted murder just might be on his mind. He hopped off that bent knee and came at her so fast even Senaé was taken aback.

"We're going to pan over to Marissa for a weather check."

His co-host's announcement had acted like water dousing fire, bringing Stanford back to the fact that his actions were on blast before a viewing audience. He'd been checked. But checking Stanford wasn't enough. The man had always been his own god.

"So, is it a 'yes' or a 'no'?"

Now, hours later in the peace and privacy of her home, Senaé recalled looking at him as if his brain had been hijacked by yard gnomes. Cognizant of where she was and that she and Stanford were providing the real show, she'd pulled him aside and lowered her voice.

"It's an 'I really need you to stop sniffing spray paint and leave me all the way alone.' Consider that your *hell no*."

She'd turned to walk back on set only to be stopped when he laid heavy hands on her.

"Ho, I will—"

"Mr. Browning, sir, can you come with us?" Obviously alerted to the possibility of Black folks acting a fool and posing a threat to peace, security manifested immediately.

"You flashlight cops better back the hell up!"

"Stanford, in my office! NOW!"

The station manager's appearance cut Stanford's okey doke completely off. Tossing a venomous look Senaé's way, he'd followed where his station manager led.

"Are you okay? Will you be able to finish the set?"

The cohost's concern was semi-authentic. Senaé swore she read a little, "I can't wait to dish this" on the face of the hazel-eyed woman.

"I'm fine. And, yes, let's do this." Shaking off the madness, she'd returned to the set, handling her business and beating that model's face as if she had spent two hours on her versus ten minutes. The results had been remarkable, touted as "doable." But Senaé knew she'd worked out her irritation through her art

and gone over and above what was achievable in a
ten-minute process. Still, she was proud of herself for
not putting her clown suit on and matching Stanford's
ignorance. It wasn't until security offered to escort her
to her vehicle afterwards that she remembered the rage
she'd glimpsed when she'd shut him down. Truth be
told, even now sitting, sipping wine and celebrating
her pending tour with her girls, mere memory produced a chill.

"Naé, where's the spinach dip?"

"Where most folks keep it, Dove. The fridge."

"Whatever, heffa. You got all this kale and foolishness in here blocking it."

"Kale is good for you. It's full of vitamins and
antioxidants."

"Yeah, and it tastes like sh—"

"Hush, Dove! Take it home since I'm leaving
tomorrow and let that kale clean your colon," she par-
ried, thankful to spend the last night before her tour
with her nearest and dearest.

"No, what I need is to get my coochie waxed like
you. You ain't the only one deserving a penis."

Ima and Lovie's wild laughter filled the kitchen as
Senaé swallowed to keep from spitting wine. "What're
you talking about?"

"Oh, please, Naé," Dove complained, placing the
bowl of dip on the tray they were loading with luscious, off-limits foods they had no business enjoying.
"You've been avoiding all questions about getting that
Mandika warrior stick since you got home. But we
know you did. Where's that slice of Bourbon Butter
cake?"

Having stashed the last slice in an overhead cabi-
net, Senaé remained silent. She planned to savor that

cake as if it were Lex.

Mine doesn't taste as good as his.

She'd meticulously followed her baby's recipe and still her end product wasn't half as good. She missed essential elements.

Mainly that man licking bourbon sauce off my assets.

Her body instantly heated with memory of their final night and fabulous farewells experienced in his bed. She'd been laying on his chest after tender but intense lovemaking, when deciding she was hungry.

"Guess that's my cue to feed you before you get hangry."

Laughing, she'd swatted his muscular, naked butt before he'd headed for the kitchen. Feeling lazy and loved, she'd sprawled in his king-sized bed enjoying the sounds of Gerald Albright caressing her skin, completely at home as if she'd found her right place in the world. When he'd returned with a loaded tray, she'd propped herself against his mound of pillows and dug in.

"Dang, you haven't changed," he'd teased when she bypassed salad and leftover shrimp scampi from dinner in lieu of dessert. "You still eat backwards."

"Not always. I just want to taste this cake you made."

"You need a little more of this bourbon sauce," he'd commented, pouring it.

"Are you tryna get me drunk?"

"Naw, baby. I simply like this cake the way I like my woman: warm and wet." Taking the fork from her, he'd scooped up a piece of the delight they were meant to share and held it out to her. A small splash of sweet, slightly caramelized sauce dripped onto her thigh in the process.

She'd reached for the napkin on the tray, but Lex bent and licked that drop of sauce, sending volleys of pleasure across her skin and pulling a moan from her

lips. Next thing Senaé knew, she was flat on her back,
Lex dribbling sauce on places pastry chefs probably didn't
intend.

"Earth to Naé!"

She came back to the present with Lovie snapping
her fingers in her makeup-free face. Wigless and without (as her granny would say) her war paint, there was
no glitz, gloss, or camouflage. Comfortable in her own
skin, simply Senaé stared out of her face. "What?"

"We were talking about you getting that stick in
Cali and not telling about it," Ima reminded. "I'm
with Dove on this one, Naé. You *did* come back walking juicy and a little wide-legged."

Lovie simply made a sound in the back of her
throat while sipping wine and looking at Senaé as if
the latter were guilty of withholding news on sexual
somethings.

Grabbing the loaded tray, she headed for her
living room and placed it on the coffee table before
plopping onto the sofa. With a pita chip, she scooped
up savory dip. "If you cows have business, mind it."

"Your business *is* ours to mind. So, spill the tea,
and tell us how Mr. Ryde-the-Knight rides. Is he still
good, Naé?" Dropping onto the sofa beside her, Dove
put a hand on Senaé's thigh and massaged, suggestive-
ly. "Do thoughts of him make your stuff vibrate? Did
y'all bust another waterbed?"

"Say what?" Lovie sang.

"Honey, these two were so hot and bothered back
in the day they broke Naé's bed with all their ho'ish-
ness."

"So much for things told in confidence," Senaé
muttered, shaking her head and pushing Dove's hand
from her leg.

"Well, confidentially speaking, did you bust his nut, and did he bust your stuff?" Ima questioned, leaning forward, expectantly.

Loading up another pita chip, she took her time chewing, refusing to answer her crew's invasive ignorance. "Not your business."

"OMG, Senaé, you're so selfish...but we still hope you got some and that you're keeping him."

She had. She was. And she was irritated. Her improved and mature self said give Lex time, but being unable to connect with him throughout the day had her feeling some kind of way. Lex had never been loud, or a pop-off. Initial silence being his mode of defense when facing dilemmas, she cautioned herself not to embellish the silence following Stanford's on-air ridonculousness. Or the fact that when Lex finally did communicate, it had been via voicemail. The connection being horrible on his end, his words were garbled, indecipherable. Yet, his tone was clear, transmitting anger and concern that left her annoyed, yet appreciative. She could do without unneeded drama in the infancy of their new relationship. Unable to do without him, she cautioned herself to view the situation through his lens.

If some chick proposed to Lex, I'd come in swinging and slinging.

"I'm absolutely keeping this man," she assured, sipping wine and toying with the hem of the oversized "My 40's Fabulous" nightshirt he'd gifted.

"Seeing as how you're already dressed for bed, I guess we're not clubbing tonight."

"Lovie, my forty's too fierce for sweating out a wig with some gold-tooth-having dude grinding on my booty like that action's real. The dumb days are done."

"Meaning we're sitting here with your old ass knitting cardigans?"

"Whatever, Dove! You cows are gonna miss me."

"Not really," Ima falsified. The most sensitive of the bunch the Kenyan-American already had teary eyes at the thought. "Naé, I want a souvenir from every city this tour takes your beauty guru butt to! And not some funky keychain or T-shirt. Bring me something good like—"

"A man with an everlasting erection," Dove interjected, sparking loud laughter.

Popping up from the sofa, Senaé hurried to the coat closet, returning with three gift bags. Elegant and eggplant in color, they bore her Queen of Shades logo in silver. "How about we start with this?" She distributed gifts to a series of "ooos" and "ahhhs" that had her swelling with thankfulness.

"Oh my gosh, Naé, these bags are gorgeous!"

"Thanks, Lovie, but peek and see what's in them."

She experienced supreme, humble satisfaction at her girls' response to her brand's products. She had God and hard work to thank for every blessing, a contract with a world-renowned cosmetic company, the opportunity to travel, and a good man.

Her joy meter took a hit thinking on her inability to connect with Lex after Stanford's proposal mayhem. His earlier voicemail aside, there'd been no calls. No texts. No response to her attempts at communication, forcing her to—again—caution herself against jumping in her feelings. If he was pissed and needed a minute, he could have it. As long as she heard from him before boarding that New York-bound plane come morning.

"Naé, this lip gloss is giving me life!"

She beamed with pride. "Lovie, you like?"

"Girl, yasss," Ima sang, answering for both friends. "And this bronzer-highlighter is the business. And these mink lashes? Boss!"

Her intended response was interrupted by someone who obviously thought her front door was a drum that needed beating. "What the heck?" Irked by the constant pounding, she marched to the door—forgetting caution and snatching it open.

"Darling, can we talk?"

She had a temporary pause before retorting, "No, but you can kick bricks, Stanford." The door would have slammed in his face but for his pressing against it as if anticipating the action. *What the?*

"Senaé, I only need a minute."

"I don't have one to give."

"Naé, you okay?"

She didn't have to glance over her shoulder to know her B.F.F.s were at her back. "I'm good. Just getting a fool out of my face."

"Senaé, sweetheart, hear me out. I caught you off guard proposing this morning without taking your ring size or diamond preference into consideration. I'll exchange it for whatever you want, so don't hold my shopping choices against me."

His ignorance was amazing.

"You seriously think my declining you is about a ring? Stanford, think again. But when you think it out, do it on someone else's doorstep." She attempted to close the door; again, he countered, pushing it open.

"Oh, hell no, Negro! Where's my phone? I feel the need to dial the PoPo," Dove threatened, heading for her purse on the sofa.

"Stay your ghetto ass out of this!"

"Little glassy-eyed bitch, this ghetto ass will whip yours, then tutor you on how to handle that bed business so you're worth your woman's two whole minutes."

"Dear Jesus!" Senaé was forced to physically come between the two. "Dove, enough!"

"Yeah, go sit down, hood rat."

She couldn't help noticing Stanford's fake New England accent had completely disappeared, leaving him in full-blown street mode. "And you! Go home, *Stan*. You smell like weed and whiskey."

"Nothing wrong with libation and lifting."

"Ima, dial 9-1-1 'cause right now I have zero time and tolerance—"

"Okay, okay! Listen, Senaé, we're good together... and I need a *classy sister,*" he emphasized, glaring at Dove, "to help polish my reputation and get me back in good standing with my public. What better way to accomplish that than a successful marriage? You're blowing up in the beauty world. That can boost my cred and visibility. You: beauty mogul. Me: national news anchor and celebrity. The press'll eat us up—"

"Is he on crank or crack? And you're local. National is a long way off."

"Lovie, please." She'd reached her limit. Her voice was flat. "Mr. Browning, you have less than two-point-two seconds to remove yourself from my property. Stay where you are and see if I'm playing."

He continued as if his foolery was fabulous, and her English needed translation. "Reel it in and listen, Senaé! I'm in trouble with my station manager *despite* ratings going through the roof after our on-air proposal. The idiot put me on disciplinary probation thanks to the negative press that thot generated, accusing me of sexual misconduct. He doesn't seem to get it. Negative or not, it's press. You been following it?"

His crooked smile gave her serious chills. Leaving him guarded by her girls, she grabbed her purse from the coat closet, quickly returning with pepper spray and a pointy self-defense mechanism.

Seeing her seriousness, his behavior flashed from cajoling to indignant. "Oh, so this is how it is? I give you your best ever sex and you give me flack."

"You gave me aggravation. My vibrator finished what you didn't. Now, step."

His crazed cackle was that of an imbalanced man. "Hanging with hood rats and that Lexington Ryde you snuck off to California with clearly has you confused."

His mention of Lex caught her off guard, but she said nothing.

"Yeah, you didn't know I knew about him, huh? Social media snitches on bitches. I called him, but never could get his ass on the phone."

"Called him, why?"

"To tell him were we were getting married. No more of this acting a pitiful bitch buying ass at an auction."

Angrily aiming pepper spray, she froze when Stanford pulled his own concealed weapon, pointing a gun in her face. Shocked, her self-defense implements dropped, granting him opportunity to lock an arm about her neck and turn her so that her back was against him.

Staring wide-eyed at her girls, Ima's screaming, *"Oh my, God!"* was the only part of the situation that felt real.

"Oh, so now I got every bitch's attention? Good!" Pressing that pistol against her head, his words were raw and rough, decorated with flying spittle. "I was nothing but good to you, Senaé. Now, you acting brand new after getting your nympho ass waxed by some California, big dick nigga? Get over it, and get used to this, Senaé. You're not his."

"Put the gun down, Stanford. Please," Ima pleaded as Lovie reached for her purse.

"Get away from that phone, and every bitch shut the hell up!" he screamed, aiming his weapon at Lovie. "Call five-oh if you want. You can all be dead before they get here. Am I clear?"

Silently nodding, Senaé's anger had her entire body shaking.

CHAPTER TWELVE
Lex

Intuition. Suspicion.

Call it what you will, but he couldn't convince himself that the crazy he saw wasn't real. Pissed and distracted over that fool's shenanigans, his initial reaction was wishing up supernatural abilities to reach through the television and choke a fool for posting up on his woman. Possessing no such superhuman skills, he'd sat wide-legged on his bed in stunned, angry silence unable to take it all in.

He couldn't process it.

Were they or weren't they exclusive? Had he misinterpreted the value of their new and improved relationship, her intent towards them? Livid, he'd had to admit a measure of his rage was directed towards Senaé for allowing that idiot in her face. And for failing to disclose she had a wannabe fiancé. Simply put, he'd felt played.

Chest-deep in his feelings, he'd been absolutely unfocused during the Black Chamber breakfast to the point that he excused himself before its conclusion.

Trying to conduct business at A Royal Ryde was worse. Untamed images of another man proposing to the woman he wanted ran amuck, leaving him close to crazy in a place he considered sanctuary.

Crazy.

In the privacy of his office, his mind circled back

to that thing he couldn't deny seeing. It had been on blast, in living color on that T.V. The truth of it had simmered beneath hurt and rage, begging attention all morning.

I know that look…

That glassy, bright-eyed staring that switched to glaring; the tilted head and vacuous grinning. With working ties to the entertainment industry, he'd witnessed a fair share of drugged out and zany. But his own personal, painful experiences outweighed each: he'd been granted first row seats to his mother's episodes more times than he cared admitting. Finding that eerie familiarity in Stanford Browning was a fist in the face. He couldn't ignore the notion: the man was certifiably insane. But something about Browning's imbalance seriously differed from his mother's.

His is lethal. As in kill himself or someone else.

Fear hit like a hurricane. He couldn't ignore, or reason it away.

"Call Senaé."

When his phone completed the command, putting him in voicemail land *again*, he'd opened his office door, hollering like love depended on it.

"Kayla!"

Putting his administrative assistant into action, the past pressed in on him. When his first love was broken by the loss of their child, he'd stepped away. Emotionally. Mentally. He'd failed Senaé before, but refused to distance himself again. Packing his firearm and permit in its case, he had no proof of Browning's intent other than a gut feeling. But the gut was enough. He followed it.

Now, one seriously delayed flight later and near midnight Central Standard Time, Lex split his attention between praying, battling to believe she was okay, and cursing slow-moving drivers to get "the hell out the way."

Answer the damn phone, Senaé!

Earlier in the day, she'd blown things up, texting, leaving multiple messages. The past few hours? Dead silence.

The sudden vibrating of his phone had him snatching it up as if heaven had heard his pleas. *"Senaé?"*

"No, Lex, baby. It's me."

A cold tremor rushed his veins at the somber sound of his foster mother's voice. "What's wrong, Mama Peaches?"

"Son...I need to talk to you. About Senaé."

His managing to pull curbside without wrecking anything was God's miracle gift to him.

"Baby, I don't know how to say this other than to say it."

Praying against the worst, her deep breath had him holding his.

"I'm partially why Senaé left back then."

It took a moment to process that Mama Peaches' lament was past tense. That fact provided temporary relief only. "Mama P., no disrespect, but I'm dealing with a serious situation."

"I know that, son, and it's partially my doing."

"No, ma'am, it's something—"

"Lexington, I'm speaking. You're listening. Now... sometimes it's hard for us seasoned citizens to admit our ways aren't the best, but I saw the proof at that auction. You and that girl are still in deep love, and that's had me walking around these past few weeks feeling like a Grade-A fool for meddling. I thought it best back then, but seeing the other side of the coin now, I admit if I hadn't persuaded her to leave you two might've fought your way through and managed to stay together."

"Ma'am?"

"Senaé left after…the baby…and your accident because of my bad advice. She came to me crying, asking how to help you. All I could think was how young and broken you both were. And, since I'm on a truth-telling mission, I didn't exactly take to her when you first brought her home." Protective, she'd thought Senaé "fast-tailed and wild," merely interested in his pro-ball potential elevating her pockets. "When she came up pregnant, folks gossiped about that baby not being yours. I knew better. You liked fast cars, but that old soul southern boy in you kept you from caring for floozies. I grew to love her, but I chose between you two. You were my first foster and my allegiance was with you so… Lex, I helped her leave."

Hearing Mama Peaches admit her part in their demise, he was unsure if he was shaking out of anger or relief that her call hadn't conveyed something horrific happening. His foster mother's revealing she'd funded their divorce and given his young wife bus fare to Dallas and seed money to jumpstart a new life left him numb.

"You'd fought hard to overcome too many obstacles. And seeing you in that hospital bed and how you took to drinking afterwards had me afraid your spiral wouldn't finish until you'd lost every gain. So…yes…I made bad decisions. Instead of being the backbone you both deserved, I helped Senaé think leaving would give you both the fresh start you needed. Son, that there is my greatest regret. I beg your forgiveness."

His heart pricked at the tears in her tone.

"She was a lovely girl, Son, but she's a lovelier woman. If you two've reconnected, I thank God for it."

Rubbing his eyes, head pressed against the headrest of his rental vehicle, he exhaled before pulling back into traffic. "Mama Peaches, I appreciate you being one-hundred with this. We can take a deeper dive at a later time, but right now I need you to do something for me."

"Absolutely."

"Pray, please."

An erratically parked car—driver's door open, headlights on—escalated his heightened alarm. Safety and security were benefits offered his clientele that required his calm. But this wasn't work; it was life and love. Hand on the gat at his back, he approached with stealth and utter silence.

"Bitch, I will end you! Your career. Your world. Yours and his! You understand this? It's me or him!"

His body went cold hearing Stanford Browning's screamed threats.

Finding the front door ajar, he crouched low, noiselessly approaching and praying. He'd never prescribed to violence, but Senaé was that woman he'd do *whatever* for; and the streets of Chi-Town had taught him to take care of his.

"It's Lex all day. You can't change that in this life or the next."

Senaé's response would've had his heart any other time, but right then it seemed cavalier considering the menace in the midst. Undoubtedly, she'd trigger a bastard as bent as Browning. Like black lightning, Lex shot forward intent on intercepting the threat.

Women whirled, gasping at his entrance, leaving him stuck and staring at what had to be a scene from a comedy.

"What the...?"

Mama Peaches and Miss Geraldine, dressed in bathrobes—the former sporting a headwrap, the latter an ever-faithful wig—sat astride Stanford Browning's sprawled, duct tape-bound body. Face down, legs and arms trussed like a chicken on its way to becoming Sunday dinner, in another life Lex might've felt for him.

"Lex?"

Stunned, he barely caught her when, projectile-like, Senaé threw herself into his arms.

"Lexington Ryde, put that gun away before you accidentally shoot somebody!"

Engaging the safety, he obeyed Mama Peaches before hugging Senaé as if he'd never see her again.

"Baby, what're you doing here?"

"Yeah, 'baby'," Browning hollered. "You flew all this way to shoot me? *Well, pull the trigger, nigga!*"

Mama Peaches slapping Browning on the back of his head had the women snickering. "I already told you we don't allow all that nasty talk here."

Struck by the ludicrousness of the scene, Lex held onto his woman with relief. "BoBo, what the hell—" He changed his approach at Mama Peaches' censoring look. "What's going on?"

Treated to a verbal replay of the entire escapade, he didn't know if he should knock Browning the hell out, or dap these women for handling him. Senaé's binding him in duct tape and Mama P. and Miss Geraldine arriving, sitting on him when he "got to foul-talking and wiggling like he wanted outta here" would have him laughing later. Right then he was close to livid. "What if that gun hadn't been plastic?"

"It was," Dove, confirmed, looking smug as she aimed Browning's realistic-looking piece at the ceiling. "I've been with enough hoodlums to know real from play. That's why I punched this fool in the face and knocked him out for holding this mess against my girl's head."

"He what?"

"Lex!" It took Senaé and her girl, Lovie, to physically restrain him from going in on the maniac. "Don't even."

Senaé's caution and the sound of sirens nearing put him on pause. "Baby, let me put this somewhere." Licensed and bonded or not, he was disinterested in law enforcement entering the premises and triggering on an armed, but innocent, Black man. Following her instructions, he secured his piece in a shoebox in a closet before rejoining the circus happening in her house.

To Lex, Browning looked as if he belonged hand-cuffed in the back of a squad car.

"Should've stayed your black ass at home," he growled.

Senaé's allegation of intent to harm now kept company with preexisting outstanding warrants for aggravated assault and sexual misconduct.

"He works in a very accessible position, so tell me how he eluded those warrants."

"Facts are stranger than fiction, Lex."

"I guess." An arm about her waist, he escorted

his love back indoors where women were grabbing belongings and exiting.

"Well Lex, baby, my work is done," Mama Peaches declared, hugging him. "When you asked me to pray, I figured I'd do one better and get on over here with my blessed oil and lay hands on whatever the situation was. Good thing we came, too." She patted her hips. "All this helped hold him down 'til the cops came."

"Peaches, I tell you what," Miss Geraldine inserted, twisting her wig. "Sitting on that boy like that reminded me I haven't been on a man in a minute."

"Jesus!" Grabbing her best friend, Mama Peaches hurried them out the door. "Senaé, when you finish traveling, we'll talk about forgiving this old woman."

"You're already forgiven."

Releasing Senaé temporarily, he was gratified by the women he loved embracing.

Ensuring the exiting parties reached their vehicles safely, he allowed Senaé to lock the door behind them.

"Whew!" She leaned against it. "The utter insaneness! I don't object, but, Honey, why'd you fly here?" she asked, touching him as if convincing herself he was real.

"Taking care of my everything." He cupped her face. "I didn't like what I saw on that T.V.—"

"Do you think any of that was real to me?"

"I'm talking about more than that whack-ass proposal, BoBo. I'm talking about the crazy. I'm blowing up your phone and you're not answering—"

"You were worried?"

"I was."

"I apologize. My battery's dead…and I lost my phone charger again."

"Senaé, really?"

She kissed his jaw as if an apology.

His facial muscles twitched, angrily. "If that mufu had hurt you—"

"He didn't. So, don't." She punctuated each word with a kiss. "I'm safe, sound...and sexy."

"*Damn* sexy," he agreed, kissing, touching her with want and relief. Hands wandering beneath her nightshirt, he caressed the naked skin waiting on him, until they were both breathing heavily. When she took his hand, he gladly followed her down the hall to her bedroom. "Wait! What's this?" Peeping a second bedroom where Styrofoam heads sat on shelves consuming an entire wall, he paused.

"My world of wigs."

Examining them, he snatched a waist-length unit the color of bright, red roses. "You got shoes to match?"

Laughing, she entered her bedroom ahead of him.

"I'm serious, bae. Grab 'em and let's do this."

"I have to be at the airport early in the morning, Lex."

"Sleep on the plane, baby. This time is mine," he decided, hands on her hips, moving them both towards her bed. "I love you, and we're doing it right this round. Bank on that." He palmed her hips while sucking her neck in a place and a way he knew would make her wet. "Ride or drive?"

Her swiveling so that his back was to the bed and pushing him down onto it, was her answer to his question of her position preference. Her discarding her nightshirt and donning that red wig had him thickening as she straddled him, and placed his hands on her bare breasts.

"Ryde...baby...for life."

EPILOGUE

Lex & Senaé
Three Months Later...

"How's my baby?"

"Exhausted as a mufu," he managed around a yawn. He'd been up since four a.m., chauffeuring a client to Santa Barbara where he'd spent the day engaged in his client's business before heading home again. Now, well after midnight, he was beyond tired. "I'm dragging too much to even take the Town Car to the lot. This puppy's parking in my garage tonight. How's Detroit?"

"Hot."

He laughed. "BoBo, bring your fine behind back to Santa Monica and let me dip it in the ocean."

"I'd rather be dipped into by you," she purred, detonating tremors in his belly.

"Yeah that, too." Proud of her success, he unequiv-ocally supported her six-city tour that had—thanks to its popularity—been extended. But this long distance, inconsistent sex, commuter relationship required creativity and discipline. Burning and yearning, he'd already flown out, connecting with her on the tour, twice. The more prolonged her absence, the more pro-nounced the fact that he needed her in his daily life.

"Did you like the cookies?"

Custom-ordered sugar cookies featuring an edible image of A Royal Ryde's logo had arrived two days ago and had already been devoured. "For sure! The crew scarfed them down. Now stop changing the subject."

"Those cookies are my new crave!"

"Yeah, okay. Three more weeks and you're finished, right?"

"Well…no and yes."

Turning onto his street, he quietly sighed, prepared for unpleasantness. "Meaning?"

"The tour's ending." She paused for dramatic effect. "But I've been offered a pop-up shop."

"What? My baby's a boss! So, where? Southside? Downtown? Bronzeville?"

"Not exactly…"

Her hesitation not lost on him, he depressed the garage door opener. Religiously, he backed his vehicles in so they'd be ready to roll the next day, but he was too tired for even that small execution. Waiting on the door to fully ascend, he called her name. "Senaé? Where's the pop-up?"

"Farther west."

He opened his mouth for clarification, but the door's full ascension left him speechless. He had to deal a minute with the unbelievable vision of his woman sitting sexy atop his AMG, flower petals sprinkled about her body. *"What…the…?"*

"West…as in Hollywood."

Parking and turning off the engine, he slowly exited, his disbelief massive. "Tell me I'm hallucinating."

"You're not."

Tiredness gone, his walk was a stalk, leading him to her luxuries. Rocking a burgundy wig, rhinestone stilettos, and barely-there, baby blue lingerie, she was his everything. In disbelief, he trailed a finger down her leg as if touching was believing.

"Hey, baby." Her whisper was sultry. "Kayla let me in when she picked up Jazz."

Kissing and lifting her, he wrapped her legs about his body, so that they were face-to-face as he made a beeline for his bedroom, clear that telling her he'd enrolled in a community college course could wait until afterwards.

Effortlessly, she responded in kind. "I miss you, Lexi Lex," she whispered when his kisses moved to her neck.

"I miss you, too. Marry me."

Arms about his shoulders, she pulled back. "What?"

"Marry me. Again," he requested, kicking his bed-room door open. The sight of flower petals, candles and a tray in the middle of his bed put him on pause only temporarily. He moved forward, clear on his destiny.

"Lex, don't play with me."

"Do I look like I'm playing?" he asked, easing her onto the bed.

Studying the warmth of his eyes, she shook her head. "You're sure? One-thousand percent?"

"To infinity on this."

"Good, because…" Wiggling out of his hold, she reached for the tray, offering him a sugar cookie beautifully decorated in pink and blue. She bit the opposite end. "We're pregnant."

Kneeling above her, he was stuck. "Huh…what? *Wait!* Hold the phone. You can't…"

Her smile was pure bliss. "Apparently, doctors don't know everything. A little Ryde is happening." Cradling his face, she kissed him sweetly before plac-ing his hand on her belly. "We're having our baby."

Now Available...
DISTINGUISHED GENTLEMEN

SUGGESTED DISCUSSION QUESTIONS

1.   How would you describe Senaé's character?

2.   How would you describe Lex's character?

3.   What attributes were most appealing or most annoying to you about our heroine and hero?

4.   Do you think Lex and Senaé's first marriage would have succeeded had they been older and more mature at the time? Why or why not?

5.   What are your thoughts about Mama Peaches' role in the failure of their marriage?

6.   What do you think of "second-time-around" romances?

7.   What effects did the motorcycle accident have on Senaé?

8.   What were the effects of the motorcycle accident on Lex?

9.   Both Lex and Senaé experienced pain because of their mothers. Discuss each situation and how it impacted our hero and heroine.

10. How did their fathers influence or affect their lives?

11. In The Birthday Bid, we get to see Senaé's inner circle of friends. Describe and discuss them.

12. Other than his bond with Khaleed and Adrian, Lex's friendships aren't depicted. Why do you think this is?

13. What skills or attributes do Senaé and Lex possess that can help their new marriage be a success?

14. What scene(s) did you find most heartwarming?

15. In what ways did colorism negatively impact Senaé's psyche? How did she overcome this?

16. In what ways did Lex's dyslexia shape him?

ACKNOWLEDGEMENTS

We already know: I couldn't do any of this without my Abba Father Most High! Thank You, Lord for the gift of putting words on paper in a way that causes others to emote and smile.

I appreciate my husband and children for their unending support and their tolerance of me and all of my zany ways and artist idiosyncrasies.

Thank you Book Euphoria for inviting me to participate in the Distinguished Gentlemen series. It's been an honor.

To all of the book promoters, book clubs, book stores, and community activists who constantly make space for authors like me to spread our wings—Georgia "Mother Rose" West and Underground Books, Dr. David Covin and the Sacramento Black Book Fair, Deborah Burton Johnson and Turning Pages Book Club, P. Mia Bailey and Crystal Bowl Book Club, Carla Mathis and Art & Soul—thank you!

SPECIAL THANKS

Adrian Porter, proprietor of Porter Transportation, Inc. (Chicago, IL): you were so gracious and generous in sharing your thirty-plus years of expertise in the transportation business. Your insight helped guide my understanding of my hero's profession. Lex and I thank you!

My beloved daughter whose multiple nicknames, include "BoBo": I knew exactly who could school me on the life of a beauty ambassador. Thank you for patiently answering my "fifty-eleven" questions as only a wonderful daughter can. Senaé and I thank you!

WONDERFUL READERS...

Thank you for being the backbone of the literary community. Without your support, writers' works would collect dust and go unnoticed. So, I thank you for noticing me!

I have a secret to share: I absolutely love hearing from and interacting with readers and book clubs in person, online, or virtually. Let's connect via any of the following:

EMAIL: sdhbooks@gmail.com
FACEBOOK: Author Suzette Harrison or Suzette D. Harrison Books
GOODREADS: Suzette D. Harrison
INSTAGRAM: suzetteharrison2200
NEWSLETTER SIGN-UP: www.sdhbooks.com
PINTEREST: Suzette D. Harrison Books
TWITTER: @Ariasu62
WEBSITE: www.sdhbooks.com
YOUTUBE: Suzette Harrison
And let's not forget virtual engagement via methods such as Skype or Facetime!

If you enjoyed The Birthday Bid I'd be honored if you'd share that enjoyment by posting a review on Amazon.com and/or other venues such as Goodreads. If you're using a Kindle, the app lets you post a review when finishing the book. How cool and convenient is that? So, please take a brief minute to share your perspective. Your review can be as brief as a sentence, but it has tremendous impact. I appreciate you doing so in advance. And by all means, please tell a friend!

Thank you for joining my journey. Until next time…

Blessings & peace,

Suzette

T-SHIRT WEARERS!

Check out my new fashion line especially designed with us readers and writers in mind!

Where Fashion Meets Fiction

www.getlitsis.com

ABOUT THE AUTHOR

Suzette D. Harrison, a native Californian and the middle of three daughters, grew up in a home where reading was required, not requested. Her literary "career" began in junior high school with the publishing of her poetry. While Mrs. Harrison pays homage to Alex Haley, Gloria Naylor, Alice Walker, Langston Hughes, and Toni Morrison as legends who inspired her creativity, it was Dr. Maya Angelou's *I Know Why the Caged Bird Sings* that unleashed her writing. The award-winning author of *Taffy* is a wife and mother who holds a culinary degree in Pastry & Baking. Mrs. Harrison is currently cooking up her next novel...in between batches of cupcakes.